A WAREHOUSE, A WITCH DOCTOR, AND A WEDDING

Deanna Oscar Paranormal Mystery Book 9

CC DRAGON

A Warehouse, a Witch Doctor, and a Wedding
(Deanna Oscar Paranormal Mystery 9)
Copyright © October 2018
By CC Dragon
Cover art by Rebecca Poole
Edited by Mary Yakovets
Proofed by: Angela Campbell

Chapter One

"DE, YOU HAVE TO HELP," Frankie nagged.

My brother had thrown himself into the supernatural learning world, which was good.

He failed to understand that forcing or controlling the supernatural backfired a lot, which was bad.

I'd barely made it to the kitchen for breakfast and Frankie was playing that broken record. He'd lost a lot of interest in marketing. We now both knew he'd been using it as a way to avoid his gifts, focusing on anything but his powers.

Tish, my cat, curled around my ankles as I got my first cup of coffee.

"I'm not letting go of this," Frankie insisted.

"Frankie, please. Rita is in physical therapy. It'll work," I argued.

Rita, the tour guide from our last big case, had been injured. The docs had been hopeful about her walking again, but my brother had also had a vision that I would be the one to heal her.

We walked into the dark and seemingly never-ending dining room of my New Orleans mansion in the Garden District and found Ivy and Brody with a ton of brochures.

"What's all this?" I asked.

The couple wanted to get married soon but I was trying to dodge too much direct help because I lacked the party planning gene. I didn't hate parties but I didn't care what color the napkins were, what sort of party favors were chosen, or what was on the menu.

Okay, maybe the menu, but it wasn't my party so I shouldn't get to pick the food. That was just good manners. Honestly, I'd never had bad wedding cake.

"Honeymoon. De, you've traveled a lot more than I have. Hawaii or Paris?" Ivy asked.

"She's going to side with you," Brody argued.

"She doesn't know which I want," Ivy replied.

I smiled. "I've never been to either place so I can't help. I haven't traveled much since I moved here so anything I know is probably out of date."

"Diplomatic," Frankie whispered.

I smiled. My brother's confidence had ticked up. It was evident in his relaxed demeanor and recent exploration of the city.

"Greg may have been there. Ask him," I suggested.

"Priests have the money to travel?" Brody asked. "He's Ivy's cousin anyway, he'll side with her."

I shrugged. "He trained at the Vatican so he probably did a side trip to France and around Europe. Hawaii, maybe not."

"Ivy, tell De to go to the rehab home and heal Rita," Frankie said.

Ivy and Brody shared a look.

Slowly, Ivy stood in her pumpkin spice-colored sundress. Fall had fallen but it meant little in southern Louisiana. She led Frankie a few feet away deeper into the dining room. "Frankie, I love the more outgoing and involved you. It's great. But you need to get that while we love the idea of De as a prophet or a miracle worker, it's a bit too Biblical. She doesn't like those kinds of labels. It's come up before and it freaks her out."

"I'm right here. I can hear you," I reminded them.

"De, come on. You know things. You see the future. It's prophetic. It's not like you're casting spells or trying to conjure the info," Brody pointed out.

"It's to stop evil people or demons doing bad things. I'm not waking up with the ten commandments. Let's not veer into the area of rules or miracles," I replied.

Frankie sighed. "But you could try. You promised you would."

Sure, I'd promised a lot of things when my brother crashed my date.

"There is a lot of work to do to get you up to speed. It was your vision. Maybe you're the healer. Our gifts won't be carbon copies of each other," I explained.

I sat in one of the old high-back mahogany chairs with a velvet cushion and flipped through the brochures. "You won't need passports for Hawaii."

"Crap, I don't have one. I've never left the country. That could take a while," Ivy said.

"Winner, Hawaii." Brody smiled.

Ivy sighed.

I bit my lip. "You can always plan for Paris on your one-year anniversary. Time to get the passports and plan the trip in detail. That's a lot more shopping."

"Fine. Lots of shopping. Okay, we're off to check some venues," Ivy said with a sly grin.

"Seriously? What about the garden you'd planned on?" I asked.

"My wedding. I want the right vibe. I want to decorate however I want and not to have to deal with weather or bugs. Let me look." Ivy was changing her mind daily about the wedding plans.

"Sorry, I just hate to see people going poor off a wedding. Save the money for Hawaii and Paris," I said.

Frankie rolled his eyes at me and continued our previous line of conversation as if I hadn't tried to change the topic. "I've tried laying hands on Rita. I'm not juiced."

I laughed. "You're scaring me a little."

"Just try. Believe you can do it and see. You think religion can help your rehab patients."

"Fine, you drive. Please remember, religion can help but that doesn't mean modern medicine is bad. God made doctors and science." I dragged myself from the comfy old chair and followed my brother to his car.

"You sound like Greg." Frankie started the car.

Twenty minutes later, we were at the physical rehab facility. Rita was sitting in a chair and using some free weights to strengthen her arms.

"Hi." She smiled when she saw us. "So nice of you to visit."

"How are things going?" I asked.

She shrugged. "I feel some tingles in my back but they say it's slow going. It'll take time. Spinal injuries are tricky."

"I want her to try," Frankie said.

Rita looked down. "Frankie."

"Faith matters. If you don't believe, it's not worth trying." I shot my brother a look. "Or putting her through it."

"But if you have the power—" he began but I cut him off with a look.

"I have no powers. How many times do I have to drag you to Heaven to make you see? The powers, the gifts, and all of it come from there. Your ego will get you killed or worse," I said.

"Worse?" Rita asked.

"Hell is worse. Death isn't so bad if you land in Heaven." I sat on the freshly made bed. It was a small room but clean and set up properly for someone with mobility issues. The open window let in fresh air and sunshine.

"If I get stuck in a wheelchair, it's no one's fault," Rita said.

"Oh, I'd blame the demons. That plantation meant a lot to you but your boss has to deal with the supernatural beings there. He absolutely can't let people use that barn for satanic worship and act like it'll all sort itself out. Those kids opened doors to new demons of all sorts. It'll take months for the monks to thoroughly cleanse the plantation."

"Dustin is working on it. Darla is on him," Rita affirmed.

"Good." I was relieved. Dustin and Darla were siblings who'd inherited the antebellum plantation where Rita had been injured giving a tour. Haunting tours could be dangerous and Dustin had been letting things just happen. "If you want to go back there and keep giving tours and telling the truth about history—you need to be able to walk. You really need it to be safe." I felt a tingling and Rita's guardian angel appeared.

I looked over and my angel was there as well.

"Angel summits freak me out," I said.

"What?" Rita and Frankie said.

"Shhh," I replied. I focused my attention back on my brother. "I'm glad you're having faith in your visions now but it's not the only component. Rita's faith and mine are really the deciding factor. Doubt is one of the biggest obstacles to success with anything and humans are infected with doubt," I warned.

I knew I was the only one that could see the angels, but Rita was looking around. Tears began to fall from her eyes. She could feel their presence, which required powerful belief.

"She's shaking," Frankie whispered.

"I don't want to die," Rita said.

"Death isn't here," I assured her.

My angel stared at me. Amy wasn't very chatty.

I looked to the other angel who finally spoke. "Her faith is there if you will be the conduit."

I could ask a million questions about why they needed a conduit. I knew they didn't. There was a point to it and I apparently didn't need to know. Maybe I'd never know. Faith.

Sighing, I hopped off the bed and reached a hand between Rita and the chair. I felt the heat as soon as I touched her skin at the small of her back. Frankie should be here doing this. It was his vision. Baby steps; at least he was more willing now. He had his own calling and his own talents. We weren't the same. But I had to make sure he was trained and knew how to handle things. Fumbling around like I'd learned was hard.

My mind continued to fixate on my brother and I realized I was channeling part of him. I saw through his eyes

Rita standing and walking. I felt the shattered pieces of her spine slide back into place, to heal and restore. His vision of healing fueled my touch and only when the heat faded did I pull my hand away.

"Your hand is hot. I can feel it," Rita said. Her voice sounded like she was somewhere far away.

"Did you fix it?" Frankie asked.

I shrugged. "I'm not a medical doctor. God made everything, it's up to him to fix it."

My hand ached a bit, like an arthritic claw. I had to sit down from the drain on my energy. Slowly, I rubbed the back of my neck. I had no idea how long I'd been standing there. It didn't feel that long to me, but my body told me something else.

"I feel different." Rita pushed on the arms of the chair.

"Wait, don't rush it," I said. I didn't expect the healing to be magically instant. There might be stiffness or pain. Human bodies were amazing but also imperfect.

She shook her head and slowly stood up.

"Told you," Frankie said.

"It feels so good." She took a step.

"Don't strain yourself. Take it easy," I suggested.

The door creaked and a nurse walked in. "What's all the ruckus?"

"I'm better," Rita said.

The nurse's jaw fell open and it was a moment before she could speak. "I'll get the doctor, we need to get some scans," the nurse said before bolting down the hall.

Rita went back to the chair. "I want to go home now."

"You'll have to be scanned before they release you. Unless you go AMA," I replied.

Frankie rolled his eyes. "It's dumb. You did it."

"We did it. Greg is going to be pissed he missed this. But scans will prove you're cured and it's not just adrenaline or mind over matter." I smiled at the joy on Rita's face.

"What? Is he planning your application for sainthood? St. Deanna of New Orleans. It has a ring to it," Frankie teased.

"Hardly. Stop focusing on me and focus on yourself," I advised.

"Healing, that's pretty advanced stuff," he argued.

I shook my head. "This isn't magic. You're not Harry Potter in book one. Your gifts are yours and you can develop them and embrace them or not. There is no graduation or degree that can qualify you. Using them is all the training you get."

"I'm trying," he said.

"Next time you have a vision, you will execute it and I will watch and support you." I sat back on the bed and let the blood flow normalize. Over the years, I'd gotten good at not fainting or giving into supernatural exhaustion. But my blood sugar was dipping. "And you're buying lunch."

"Sounds like the training wheels are coming off," Rita said.

Frankie nodded. "Can you stand again?"

Rita did, with more strength this time. Frankie pulled out his phone and took a picture. "Proof."

"The world might need proof. I need a Monte Cristo sandwich and fries." I couldn't see the angels anymore—I just needed to fuel myself. It seemed too quick and easy, but it wasn't natural. Supernatural healing didn't need recovery time. There was nothing more I could do, or my brother, for that matter.

I just needed to fuel myself and rest a bit. The medical setting wasn't energizing me.

"Energy dip. Got it. We'll go. Bye." Frankie hugged Rita.

"Thanks. I just can't...there aren't words." Rita smiled. "But go. I'll be stuck getting tests for the rest of the day. Hearing the medical theories. They won't believe it's a straight-up miracle, but I don't care."

HALF AN HOUR LATER, I'D INHALED MY LUNCH AND WAS indulging in a triple chocolate sundae.

"Why did you try it?" Frankie asked.

"I saw the angels. Mine and Rita's. I realized if they were on board, it was real. If you'd seen them, I'd have made you try," I said.

"I did try," he said.

I nodded. "I know. Your enthusiasm is good. Your confidence seems up."

"Seems?" he asked.

"You need to try. To prove to yourself you can do things. Observation and exposure time are over," I said.

"I don't want anyone to get hurt because of me." He clanked his coffee cup on the saucer.

"But they will. It'll happen. You'll also save people. The main thing is to keep your ego in check. That's what the evil will feed on. If you think you do any of it on your own, you're opening yourself up to the demons."

"I wondered how you stay humble," he said.

"There is no arrival. There is no answer, Frankie. Every case is a challenge. When you think you have the hang of it, the supernatural will flip your world upside down. Eddie's illness and his soul? I was dumb enough to think the demons were coming after me through him. He had his own gifts. I won't make that mistake with you."

Frankie nodded. "Eddie likes Heaven better."

"Who doesn't?" I asked.

"I guess. It is Heaven."

I smiled. "It feels foreign to you still. That's okay. We're not meant to stay there now, not yet. Get used to being around the demons and angels and feeling out the differences. Focus on honing your skills so the next vision you get you can act on. Trust your gut. The devil will tug at your heart and confuse your brain."

"I wish I'd paid more attention in religion class," Frankie admitted.

I checked my phone. "There is always Greg. My Latin still sucks."

"Greg. I haven't seen Paul around much. I feel like I'm sucking your time up," Frankie said.

"Don't worry about it. He and I aren't working together all the time. He has a job and gets that mine varies a lot." I had to trust Paul and that we were both in it together. He got busy just like I did.

My phone binged with a text so I picked it up off the table.

Ivy: *Found a great abandoned warehouse for the wedding. Gotta be cheap to rent. Huge and we can do it cheap.*

I shook my head and texted: *Abandoned? Sounds sketchy. Find somewhere safe.*

Ivy: *My wedding.*

Me: *Sounds great then. Finger crossed it's available.*

Ivy: *I want you to see it this afternoon.*

I frowned at my phone.

"What's wrong?" Frankie asked.

"Ivy," I said.

"Weddings are stressful. We did some at the hotel. Brides are all nuts," Frankie replied.

"You're probably right." My gut said there was more, but I had to wait and get a bit more proof.

Me: *Okay. Meet you at the mansion and we'll go whenever. Back within the hour.*

Ivy: *Great, thanks!*

"You don't have to help with the wedding," he said.

"I'm a bridesmaid, of course I do. She's just picking really odd places lately. Like the plantation. I still don't get why she'd want her engagement party there. It's gorgeous and spacious but we knew how haunted it was. That's dangerous. An abandoned warehouse?" I ran the spoon around my melting half-eaten sundae.

"Warehouse? I mean, you did say don't blow the budget," Frankie agreed.

"That's a bit extreme. There are enough church halls that wouldn't cost much." I shrugged.

"More ice cream?" he asked.

I laughed. "No, I feel better. I need more info. We'll see what Ivy has in mind. You stick with Greg for a bit. Stay out of trouble."

Frankie laughed. "You're the one who tends to land in trouble."

I ate one last spoonful of ice cream. "Okay, let's go."

Frankie stared at me. "I mean it. Be careful or you'll end up in trouble. Ivy's place is not in a good neighborhood."

"Great. Let's go." I already had a feeling that the warehouse was abandoned for a reason. Hopefully it was just the location.

Chapter Two

IVY WAS SO EXCITED as we drove to the warehouse in a rough part of town that she kept telling me about her color scheme options. I wasn't the right woman to talk shades of pink with, but I did my best to act interested.

"Ivy, you want people to come here with wedding gifts and in formal dress?" I asked.

I'd come prepared. I had my gun tucked in the back of my jeans and wore nothing flashy or expensive. I wasn't much for high-end fashion anyway, but the wrong purse might just get me mugged.

"It's not that bad. The reason areas get run down is there is nothing there. No money gets put into them," she pointed out.

I nodded and found a parking spot. "I'm all for helping the local economy but one event won't matter. You're not buying it. This might be a nice rehab expansion but for a wedding? There are places that are set up to handle big events."

"Cheaper venue saves money for the honeymoon and I have plenty of male friends to help set up and decorate. This will hold more people for a lot less. Mobile bar and DJ are easy enough." Ivy hopped out and led the way. "Just be careful."

A couple of homeless people panhandled outside.

One woman had sunglasses on and her sign said she was blind. She sat by the doorway wearing a light blue dress and a dark shawl. As I passed, she grabbed my hand.

"Don't go in there," she said.

"Why?" I asked.

"It's not safe for good people in there," she said.

"Then why do you sit outside?" I got a good read on her. She really was blind and homeless but a good person. It wasn't anything demonic that had put her here.

"I warn people off of squatting there. In bad weather, people sneak in and stay. A lot of nights in the winter it gets packed. Some always end up dead," she whispered.

"We're just looking around," I replied.

She nodded and released my arm. I glanced back at Ivy, who seemed unfazed by the warning.

Clutching the spray bottle of Holy Water in my jacket pocket, I opened the door. I had the right weapons for whatever came at me.

The wall of evil hit me and suddenly I had a splitting headache. Dozens of dead turned and stared at me while demons hid or modified their appearance. Normally I felt more before I entered a place, but this building seemed to keep things under tight wraps. That door was a true threshold. Some demons flew into the walls to get away from me. I'd grown better at seeing them compared to merely feeling them or seeing dark mists.

Ivy strutted into the space in her four-inch heels and relatively demure navy dress. "It's lovely. Huge and electric."

There were no lights, but the atmosphere literally buzzed. Ivy usually didn't pick up on the supernatural stuff. She was grounded in this world.

"It's full of demons and the dead. It's not safe," I said.

"So was the plantation. Everything here is haunted. We'll never find a venue that isn't inhabited in some way," she replied.

I didn't have a great comeback for that. Most places in New Orleans did have some hauntings.

"Like it?" she asked.

I closed my eyes and went deeper. I groaned and cut off my psychic exploration. A stabbing pain seared my gut and I felt paralyzed for a moment.

"People have died here," I said.

"The lady just told us that much. Homeless people use it for shelter. People die everywhere. We can have Greg bless it or something. It's not like you'll find a totally ghost-free place," she replied.

I nodded and looked around, deciding to make wedding talk in order to buy time while I figured out what this place was hiding. "It's a nice blank canvas to decorate. How much do they want to rent it?"

"I have a call in. I'm going to come back tomorrow, Darla is going to lend me her laser measurement thing. This place is too big for a standard tape measure. Then I can make some measurements. See how many tables we can fit." She pulled out her cell phone and took some pictures.

"When did everyone get so friendly with Darla?" The woman we were referring to was co-owner of the haunted plantation where Rita worked and was also a local realtor.

Walking the huge room, I found a few signs of the occult. Some had skeletons of small animals behind them. "It needs a major cleanup first."

"Duh. That'll keep the cost down." Ivy found the light switches and flipped them. A few of the overhead lights actually blinked to life. "It has power. It'll need new light bulbs, but I think we'll do a subtle lighting with some spooky Halloween twinkle lights. Green and purple are so on theme. Isn't that the perfect day to get married?"

"You're getting married on Halloween?" I asked.

"Why not? It's a big thing here," Ivy said.

Suspicious rattling noises came from the back rooms.

"We should go," I said.

Ivy shook her head. "It's probably just some homeless people. Hopefully, there are bathrooms back there."

"No, we're going. Come back later with Gunner and Matt to measure." I noticed a very old and faded *No Trespassing* sign that was tagged with graffiti.

"Fine. If you can stand to be in here then it can't be that haunted," she pointed out.

"Or I'm getting stronger," I shot back.

We headed for the door and I locked it behind me so people stayed out.

I handed the blind woman who still sat there my card. "In case you need anything."

"How's she supposed to read that?" Ivy asked.

"Good point." I wondered.

"I have friends who can read it for me if I need it. God bless," she said.

"You too," I said.

We climbed back in the car.

"See, it can't be that dangerous for her to sit there," Ivy said.

"She's guarding it," I said more to myself than Ivy.

Back home, I found Paul going over the rehab center info. Was I late for something?

"Did I miss a meeting?" I asked.

"No, I met with the manager and things are good. Donations are up. Success rate is better than average and that's getting us more notice. The wait list is crazy." Paul had papers and his laptop at the dining room table.

I sat down. "That's good."

"What?" he asked.

I shrugged.

"You look exhausted." He put a hand to my forehead.

"I'm fine. Ivy took me to a warehouse where she wants to have the wedding. Full of ghosts and demons. It's weird. There has been violence there." I rubbed the back of my neck.

"I'll get you some coffee," he said.

"No thanks, I need some water," I said.

I went to the kitchen and grabbed a cold bottle of water. Ivy had already hustled upstairs.

"There's more to it," Paul pressed, following me to the kitchen.

"It's a crazy place. There was a woman sitting outside. Blind and homeless. I wanted to help her but she's not addicted to anything. She just needs help," I said.

"Did she ask for it?" Paul asked.

I shook my head. "Why is she sitting out there panhandling?"

"Some people make a living like that. Scammers."

"She wasn't. I don't get it." I went back to the dining room and Paul followed me once again.

Paul sighed. "Don't tell me you want to open a homeless shelter now."

"Of course not. I can't save the world. I just got a weird vibe. Then again, when do I get a normal vibe? Ivy's right. Most places in New Orleans have a haunting but this place. I don't get why anyone would want a wedding there," I said.

"Maybe she wants it for a club? That much space would work for a new club. Depending on the zoning—maybe she's thinking of expanding that business?" Paul suggested.

"If she is, I'm not. She can branch out on her own. I don't need more clubs." I took a long drink of water.

"Good, we're already stretched too thin. My job and yours plus the rehab centers. Owning businesses is good, but we have to give them the right attention," Paul replied.

"Are you saying I'm not?" I asked.

He shook his head. "Your job is far from normal and can be draining. I'm just saying you don't need to take on more."

"I know we haven't had much time together. I feel like I'm always saying that. Maybe you should move in?" I pondered.

"Don't do that. Don't suggest things out of guilt or convenience. Relax. I have to get to some meetings. I'll email you the reports from the manager. Nothing major, just a couple of decisions need to be made. If you need my help, text me." He collected his stuff.

"Wait, you're going?" I asked.

He shrugged. "You're distracted."

I rubbed my eyes. "It's not a case, it's Ivy's wedding. That's going to be the elephant in the room until it's done."

He nodded. "I know. I can't wait to see the wedding. I love that you want to help everyone but you need to focus and say no sometimes."

"Is this about Frankie?" I asked.

Paul smiled. "It's all about you. Talk to you later."

He left and I sat there staring at the big dining room table. "Did we have a fight and I missed it?"

"Who are you talking to?" Frankie popped in from the hallway.

"Just myself. Am I a bad girlfriend?" I asked.

"You're weird but I'm finding I am, too." Frankie smiled.

He was dressed in naturally ragged jeans and a Chicago Bears t-shirt.

"You look very casual. More healing missions?" I asked.

"No, I've been thinking…" Frankie sat down. "Wait, are you and Paul okay?"

I nodded. "I think so. I don't have a normal life and he puts up with it. We all have bad days. I need to make more time for him, I think."

"You're not on a case right now, right?" he asked.

"No, not exactly. Just trying to pin down Ivy's wedding venue." I shook my head.

"Need help?" he asked.

"I might, but Greg will be easier to drag into it since he's Ivy's cousin. Right now, you seem to have plans of your own." I could see the twinkle in my brother's eye.

"Sort of, maybe. I've been thinking it might help if I had my own place. I know, it's great to be here with you and your protection. And the haunted objects and ghosts make for some hands-on learning. However, I think all the people here—they're your friends. This is your team. I want to be part of it but I really need my own space. I want privacy and my own kitchen and bathroom. This was fine in college and the mansion is cool but it's not me," he said.

"Is the mansion really me?" I asked.

He grinned. "It is. You feel like you belong here with that houseboy cleaning up for you and the gardeners. You need that support and it works. You get these weighty cases and you need people to help and you pay them well and it's all good. I'm still learning, I can find a house that isn't so paranormally infested and work on my powers and have some quiet time, too."

"You can rent your own apartment, sure," I said.

Frankie shook his head. "I feel like I'm all in my head. I want to do something with my hands."

"You want to build a house?" I asked. "Volunteer for Habitat for Humanity or something."

"No, I've been talking to Darla from the plantation case. She's in real estate. She was talking about how she sorts out haunted places. Warns people and so on. Some are dangerous, some aren't. She's starting her own agency and talked about handling devalued or trashed properties in addition to prime ones. Selling them to flippers."

"You want to flip houses?" I asked.

"One for me to start. Nothing with foundation damage. She knows contractors and maybe it could work out. Nothing super complicated but I worked construction all of the summers in college. It was good money and I know what I'm doing so I won't get screwed. If I like the finished result, I can live there. It'll take time—it's not like I'm moving out tomorrow. But it gives me something of my own," he said.

I smiled. "You're not going to run to Mississippi or Texas or anything, right?"

He chuckled. "You can check up on me anytime you want. I swear, I'll give you the address. And I'll make time to work on cases with you to keep learning. Honestly De, I don't how you just moved in here and dealt with this stuff. It's a lot."

"There were much fewer people in here. I was alone here most of the time," I admitted. "If you need help buying the property..."

"I got it. I've been working. I'm not a little kid," he said.

"I know, I just feel weird. Gran left me all of this. You have the gift, too. It's as much yours as mine." I patted his arm.

"We'll see. If I don't like the first house I remodel, I can sell it and build up some cash to buy the right place." Frankie grinned.

"Good plan. Are you looking for something that's not haunted?" I asked.

He chuckled. "Maybe that's part of the challenge? To sort out what's there and manage it. See what works for me. Some might be ghost-free but Darla said most have some stuff. Some lingering attachments."

"You'll find the right place. Don't rush. I'd rather see you flip and sell ten houses than move into a dangerous one," I warned.

"I promise. I'm going to meet with her and we're going to look at some small homes that need rehab. She's into decorating so it'll work out. Want to come?"

I shook my head. "No, this is your baby. Good luck."

"Okay, gotta go. You look tired, take a nap or something," he said.

I took another drink of water. I got that creepy feeling

that my body was being carved up again. What was going on?

And seriously! When did Ivy and my brother get so friendly with Darla?

Chapter Three

_____

TISH POUNCED on my cell phone as it chimed with a new text message. I hadn't intended to take a nap but I couldn't shake the weird energy. Rolling over in bed, I snatched the phone from my adorable black cat and got a paw on my hand in return.

"Mine," I teased.

The message was from Greg.

Greg: *I'm bringing dinner tonight. Everyone please be there at seven.*

I texted back a thumbs up. I wasn't sure what was going on with Greg but Mary Lou was helping Ivy with wedding plans.

I looked around and felt lonely. "Amy?"

My guardian angel was always there but I rarely saw her. She materialized.

"What's wrong with me?" I asked.

"Nothing," she replied.

"Was I wrong to help heal Rita?" I asked.

"If it was wrong, you wouldn't have been able to do it," she replied.

I frowned. "But demons can do things, too."

"You think a demon worked through you?" she asked.

"My brother was the one dead set on my healing this woman. It might've been a false vision," I suggested.

"Your faith is strained. You know what you need to do." Amy disappeared.

I grumbled. The angel was right. Much like a washing machine, sometimes I went off balance. My second guessing myself was good but there was only one way to recalibrate.

Closing my eyes, I projected myself and sat in the waiting room. I could go straight into Heaven but I needed to feel it all out. Here it was all about threes. Three doors were before me. Heaven, Hell, and possibly a limbo-like place for those who never were exposed to religion? I'd never been in two of them.

Hell felt as wrong and upsetting as ever. There was no draw, despite all the power and pain that oozed through the door.

Limbo felt like a void and I had no interest there, either.

I entered Heaven. Again, there were three levels. The first and main area was nice. The second area was more sparkly and powerful. Gran existed here. I moved through the level without paying attention to the people or angels around me. No one stopped me as I approached the inner-most level.

It was like getting too close to the Sun. Not in a hot way but in a powerful way—that power could burn me up. I wanted to walk right in and stay. The draw shook me. I'd never been so drawn to what they called the Throne Room. It always terrified me before.

I stood at the doorway and waited for the fear.

A trio of angels appeared. I realized they were always there but my ability to see them was conditional.

"In or out?" they asked.

Looking around, I felt oddly alone. "I need confirmation that I'm not a prophet."

The angels looked at each other but said nothing.

"Can I go in there and come back out?" I asked.

"If you are summoned," one angel replied.

"How do I know if I'm summoned?" I shrugged.

The angels shared another glance.

"You would simply be here. You would not have chosen it. You should go," they replied in unison.

"If I go in?" I asked.

"You'll be dead and judged. You must be called. You can get your answer without entering," they replied.

"How? People have called me one but I don't believe it. I healed someone but..." I rubbed my neck. "I should go."

The angels nodded and vanished.

I sat down next to the entrance and closed my eyes.

Eddie appeared and sat facing me. "What are you doing here?"

"I don't know," I confessed.

Eddie smiled. "Frankie?"

"No. Well, yes. He called me a prophet. Greg did that before. It's not true but I need to be sure."

"You just...well, you're not." Eddie frowned.

"How do I know?" I asked.

"We're all called to things. Jobs on earth, you could say. Some are parents—some aren't. Some can heal humans, and some can fight the demons. The longer you go, the more gifts you'll acquire. Prophet is a job, not a gift. You have prophetic visions but that doesn't make you a prophet," he said.

"Frankie is confused. You're right. Prophets speak for God. I'm not that," I confirmed.

"It's good, though, good to check. To ask. You never know what you might be called to one day." Eddie smiled.

"Maybe Frankie is projecting?" I suggested.

Eddie scrunched his nose. "He's still learning. He might have some healing powers or he might *want* them. Accepting that he has some powers might go to his head. I suggested he pick a more concrete project to do while he learns."

"You're the one with the house flipping suggestions. I wondered where that came from," I replied.

"He was good at construction. He's good at marketing too, but he liked the more physical stuff. Dad wanted him to have a nice comfortable office job," Eddie explained.

I nodded. "Working outside in the heat and elements wouldn't be fun for me. Our parents are pushy."

Eddie snorted a laugh. "They were. Don't put so much pressure on yourself. I can help Frankie."

"I don't know what to do with myself. I feel like things are changing but I don't know how or what to do," I admitted.

"Change is the only constant. Ride the wave and stay close. Now get out of bed. Your energy and faith are restored. You know exactly who you are and don't let anyone else make you question it." Eddie vanished.

I opened my eyes and found Tish kneading my stomach in her sleep like a baby kitten. Scratching her between the eyes, I heard her purr motor start up.

"My brother is getting really deep in his afterlife. At least he seems content and very at home there," I said to my feline friend.

Then again, he was in Heaven.

I checked the time. Nearly seven. I had to freshen up and get downstairs for dinner!

"Sorry, Tish." I shifted the cat to the bed. Instead of curling up and going back to sleep, she darted off the bed.

"Cats," I muttered. At least Tish would never be impressed with any of my gifts. The indifference of a cat was oddly comforting when people often looked at you differently.

THE SMELLS FROM THE KITCHEN DREW ME A BIT EARLIER THAN seven. I took the back stairs and nearly ran into a priest when I walked into the kitchen.

Not Greg, a strange priest in the black clothes with a white collar.

"Hi," I said.

"Hello, Ms. Oscar," he said.

"Doctor," Greg corrected. "She has a few PhDs."

"My apologies. You have a lovely home," he said.

"Thanks. You didn't say you were bringing a guest and making him cook," I said to Greg.

"This is Eli Larmine. He just got back from the Vatican where he trained in exorcism. A mutual friend recommended that he look me up," Greg explained.

"I know you've been working with the monks but that's their order, their choice to work on cases. If they piss off the bishop, not our problem. Are you sure you want to annoy the diocese, Father Larmine?" I asked.

"I want to help. I want to learn. Greg agreed to let me

shadow him and he'll mentor me. There are a few cases approved by the diocese I'm in." The priest took a pan from the oven. "Chicken with Tuscan breading and red sauce. The pasta is ready, too."

"He likes to cook." Greg shrugged.

"Italy was Heaven for food. Please, come." The priest went to the dining room with the pan.

"He's making himself at home," I said.

"He's excited. He wanted to make dinner as a thank you for letting him help and shadow. Your cases are my cases most of the time," Greg said.

"The food smells good," I said.

"You okay?" Greg asked.

I sighed. "Everyone is asking me that today. I'm fine."

We went into the dining room and it was set. Tons of rolls, pasta, salad, and food. "Wow," I said.

Frankie and Darla were there. Mary Lou and Ivy were showing Brody samples of something. Matt and Gunner were talking. Paul sat looking a bit uncomfortable.

I sat next to Paul. "Hi, how are things?"

He nodded. "What's up?"

"Dinner. A new priest to help, I guess," I replied.

"You look a bit better," he said.

"You do," Frankie jumped in. "You napped."

There was very little privacy, I got it. Frankie deserved that. So did Paul.

"I did," I replied.

The priest said grace and we started eating.

"How beautiful was Rome?" Mary Lou asked Eli.

"Amazingly beautiful. If I could stay in Vatican City I would, but I'd be helping no one there. It's so nice to help someone so gifted." He lifted his glass at me.

"How do you know I'm gifted? The Catholic church wouldn't approve. They'd call me a lot of bad things," I replied.

"No religion is perfect. I prayed. I had a vision of you. I'm where God wants me to be," Eli replied.

We ate and talked about the wedding for a bit.

"It's delicious," I said.

"Thank you. What sort of help can I be? What sort of cases are you on?" Eli asked.

I shook my head. "Nothing right now."

"De healed a woman. She's been a bit tired since but she's looking better," Frankie blurted.

"Healing. A great gift," Eli said.

"We need to start documenting this more so people know," Frankie said.

"No," I said firmly.

"New Orleans has plenty of people with gifts and all sorts of supernatural stuff. Don't worry, no one will freak out," Darla said. "I'm opening my own real estate agency specializing in haunted property."

"There. You can help her, Father Eli," I said.

"De," Greg said.

"Sorry, I'm better but I don't like to be the center of attention," I replied.

Frankie shrugged. "A prophet's curse."

I slammed my fork down. "I'm not. Stop saying that, please. I have prophetic visions and dreams but I'm not a prophet. I'm not authorized to speak for...that is very different. Healing and fighting evil, sure. Don't advertise more than I can do. It's wrong."

"Prophet or prophetic, it's words," Frankie said.

"No, it isn't just words. It's grabbing for power. Frankie,

you can't want power or you'll slide right into Hell," I warned.

He smirked.

"I'm not kidding. I'm dead serious. You have gifts most people don't. Learn to use them, don't want more. Don't let it go to your head or the demons will start granting your wishes and you'll belong to them—again." I looked around at everyone's shocked faces. "Sorry. I knew that label was wrong, but I went and I checked with some people at the top. Please don't call me something I'm not."

"Fighting evil is better than being a mouthpiece," Ivy said.

"Where did you go?" Eli asked.

I chuckled. "It's a long story."

Paul put his hand on my back. "You okay?"

I nodded. "I know my powers can grow and change but words have power and it felt wrong."

"Sorry, De," Frankie said.

I shook my head. "Just realize your words have power. We don't know everything."

"I know, I just thought…. I was proud of you. I had that vision, and I knew it was supposed to happen," Frankie said.

I smiled. "I believe you but there are a lot of different gifts we can get. Our gifts tend to be more action than preaching. I'd feel horribly wrong speaking for God. There are plenty of people called to do that."

Frankie nodded. "Cool. Until De gets a case, Father Eli, why don't you come and check out a couple of properties I'm looking at buying? They have spirits. I know that much. Help me cleanse them or make sure they're not dangerous."

"Thank you, I'd like that," Father Eli replied.

"Wow, I've been wanting to start my own business for a

while and it's finally all falling into place. Thank you," Darla smiled.

She was far more pleasant and sunny than when she was dealing with the haunting at her family's plantation.

"Sorry to change the subject but Ivy, did you get Matt to check into the building you want to have your wedding at?" I asked.

"No, but I asked Gunner to come with us tomorrow and check the dimensions. It's not a big deal. The place is abandoned, I'm sure bad things happened there. We can change that energy," Ivy said.

I shot Matt a look.

"Text me the address," Matt said.

Ivy sighed. "It's my wedding."

I looked at Greg and shook my head.

"De, I know you want my wedding in the gardens here and the gardens are lovely, but it's my wedding. I'm the bride, argument over," Ivy said.

"Ivy, it's a nice space but it's not the only place we should consider. We should have a backup. The owner hasn't responded yet," Brody said.

"It's his wedding, too," Darla said.

"You're sweet but new here," Ivy dismissed Darla's comment.

Greg's eyebrow arched.

"Maybe we could do it at my mansion? Inside so no weather worries. Plenty of room. I'm happy to do it. I love an event," Mary Lou offered.

Brody smiled.

Ivy's shoulders slumped. "I know you mean well, Mary Lou, but I don't want charity. I want to pay for my wedding myself."

"It's not charity," Mary Lou insisted.

"Pride helps no one. Gifts are good for everyone's soul," Eli said.

Ivy's posture snapped back and she gave the priest an odd look. "Would you do the honors and marry us?"

"I…I…can't," Eli managed. He took a drink of water. Apparently performing the marriage of two drag queens was outside his comfort zone.

"Then you can keep your advice to yourself and sit there disapproving of us," Ivy said.

"I didn't…I don't…" Eli put a finger up to his lips.

"Smart," Brody said.

"Ivy, even servants of the church don't agree with every doctrine. No religion is perfect," Greg said firmly.

"I know and I'm sorry, but it's my wedding. I want that warehouse. Dinner is lovely but I need to talk with Mary Lou about dresses and colors. Hopefully no one will be upset about that. Is that too much for a bride to choose?" Ivy stood up and walked away.

Mary Lou wiped her mouth with her napkin and set it on the table before she excused herself.

"I'm very sorry," Eli said.

"She's not herself," I apologized.

"Wedding jitters. It's the ultimate event. The biggest party of her life. She's the star. You know how she loves that," Brody said.

"I get that but this warehouse…" Greg shook his head.

Matt frowned at his phone. "There have been some issues at that address. Not the best area but we can hire off-duty officers for extra security."

"Not worth the fight," Brody said.

I nodded. "You're right. Let her stalk the owner to rent

it. We can hope he doesn't want to do that. Brody and Greg, maybe mention that having a backup in case the owner can't be located is a good idea. Don't say what, just have her pick a backup and maybe put a deposit on it?"

"You could always use the plantation. Since De and her group investigated, there have been a lot less attacks. Much more routine haunting, fewer injuries," Darla said.

"I'd love to hear about this case. Please, tell me more," Eli said.

"Standard poltergeist, slave ghosts, and cursed land plus teens worshipping Satan making it worse. Classic case, really." I dished out more chicken and dug in. Worrying made me hungry.

Chapter Four

"DE, WAKE UP," Ivy whispered.

I hugged my pillow tighter. It had to be a dream.

A long fingernail poked my shoulder. "De, I need you."

Grumbling, I rolled over and looked at the clock. "It's one in the morning. What's wrong?"

I felt no danger but Ivy was in full panic mode. Tish meowed and murmured as she jumped off the bed and went to curl up in a quieter part of the house.

"My reception is going to take place at night and I need to see the venue at night," she said.

"Where's Brody?" I asked.

"At the club. I took a night off to work with Mary Lou. I almost left dinner to go to the club with that priest going on and on about Vatican City. But this is important. Before I book the place, I need to see it at night," Ivy said.

"The owner contacted you?" I asked, trying to wake up.

"No, but that's just a matter of time. Think positively!" Ivy said.

"It's the middle of the night, I'm not thinking at all. Go back to bed." I tried to pull the covers over my head.

She tugged my blanket off of me. "No, you have to come. Matt and Gunner are out somewhere. They won't answer my calls."

"Out? Did they go with Brody?" I asked.

Ivy shook her head. "I texted him and checked. It doesn't matter. We can just drive by and see."

"No, that's not a good idea," I said.

"We're going or I'm going alone. I thought you were my friend," she scolded.

I sat up reluctantly. Like it or not, I was awake. "I am your friend. I'm just not obsessed with that wedding venue."

"You want me to use your gardens." Ivy crossed her arms.

I shook my head. "Any normal event venue is fine. Here, a banquet hall, Mary Lou's house. You have options. Why are you so into this one?"

"It's the one. Like I know Brody is the one," Ivy insisted.

"Ivy, I'm worried about you. It's a place. You can't get so attached to it," I warned.

Ivy sighed. "Get dressed and meet me downstairs. One little drive-by and we're done."

I wanted to believe her but I knew it wasn't true. Something was pulling her there. Ivy was normally so grounded and routine. She ran the clubs and helped with investigations by being the clearheaded one. She never saw ghosts or anything. Sure, she was theatrical and enthusiastic, but this was obsessive.

She stomped downstairs and I went into the bathroom. After freshening up my bedhead and throwing on some clothes, I emerged and found shoes as well as my purse.

My phone was charging. I disconnected it and checked the weather, grabbed a light sweater as I left the room. Trying not to wake anyone else, I made it down the long flight of stairs where Ivy was waiting.

"I'll drive," I said.

"No, I will," Ivy insisted.

I locked the house behind me and we climbed into her car. We were nowhere near tourist areas so traffic was light but there were plenty of police sirens.

As Ivy parked, I looked for the blind woman but she was gone. A couple of other people slept on the sidewalk. We tried not to disturb them.

Ivy turned off the car and got out.

"We're just driving by," I said.

"I want to see it again," she replied.

I followed her and felt the pull. The padlock that I'd specifically bolted last time was once again hanging uselessly on the hasp. Walking inside, the few lightbulbs that were still operable flickered. Nothing fled this time. There were some humans in there and they worried me more initially.

"Get out of here," an old man shouted. I could see a gray mist hanging on him. Demons messed with his life. As much as I wanted to help him, I looked over at Ivy and saw nothing clinging to her. That almost made it worse. I could handle a demon attachment. What was going on with her?

"We're just looking around," Ivy replied.

"Go before they get you!" he yelled.

I felt the demons lurking closer, but the danger wasn't them. At least not the danger the old man meant. The demons were feeding on fear and trauma of the people here, playing mind games that there was no hope and that no one cared. If I lived like this, it wouldn't be too hard to convince me of that, either. The devil was so basic in some ways but played right into human fears and doubts. The demons protected this place to keep the evil going. To keep the souls coming.

"Ivy, we should go. You've seen it," I said.

Ivy kept walking toward the back. "I want to see it all."

"With the owner, in the daylight. Ivy, now," I demanded.

Ivy turned and glared at me. "You're not the boss. Not here. This is for my wedding. Not the club. Not your mansion. My wedding. I want it my way. I am allowed to control some things."

Ivy definitely wasn't herself. "You think this is about ego? Being the boss? I'm not trying to control you. We're not safe here."

"You've gone Garden District. All mansion," Ivy scoffed. "Like I'm just your servant."

I shook my head. "You don't mean that. It's not true."

"Filthy rich and has an entourage. What was that TV show like that?" she asked in a sarcastic tone.

"Entourage? Ivy, you're working too much and not sleeping. I know weddings are stressful but...you need to take care of yourself. I don't know if it's just the wedding or a midlife crisis but you're not yourself," I said.

"I MUST BE CRAZY. DEMONICALLY POSSESSED? IT CAN'T JUST be I want to control my own wedding. I want everything the way I want it...and what would you know about weddings?" she snarked.

Ouch. "Fair enough. Let's go. Go in the back, see what's

there." I shrugged. Playing along seemed the safe move right now.

I followed very slowly. If she wanted to see bathrooms and prep rooms, I didn't care. Off to one side in an alcove was a group of homeless. The blind woman wasn't among them.

"You should go," a woman said. The woman wasn't afflicted with any mists or demonic attachments. Her concern was genuine.

"Why don't you?" I asked.

She shrugged. "We were living in our car but it got repossessed."

"I'm sorry. Maybe I can help?" I offered. I looked around her area and it wasn't filthy. The warehouse overall wasn't the disgusting rat-infested place I'd imagined. It wasn't clean by any means, but it wasn't disgusting. It felt abandoned and overrun with ghosts. They were silently pulling at me, but I'd learned to tune out the simple human dead who chose to linger.

The demons were more of a threat and Death did its part to collect souls. Once the bigger issues were handled, the human dead could be released and cross over. Normally, if they remained something kept them there. Even in death it was obvious that their time among the living had been hard; their souls, though translucent, looked worn and haggard. In this instance they huddled in a group in the middle of the warehouse floor, peering around uncertainly while the humans camped along the walls of the building.

"Go, they always take one. You need to go," she said.

"They?" I pressed.

I felt the presence of more humans rolling up, out back in the alley.

Running to the back, I grabbed Ivy by the arm and dragged her out front.

"There's a body!" she cried.

As we approached the door, police burst in.

"Hands on your head!" one shouted.

"Get on the ground!" yelled another officer.

Behind us, the homeless scattered out the windows and back doors. Whoever was in the alley also had burned rubber to get away.

"There's a body back there." Ivy pointed.

"We were just looking around," I said.

"Shut up, we need to secure the building," one officer said.

A body? Had those men in the alley dumped it? I hadn't felt someone freshly dead when I walked in. I wanted to call for Death and ask but right now that would only make me look crazy—even by New Orleans standards.

The ghosts and demons had the police nervous and twitchy. For now, I was going to keep quiet and wait for things to calm down.

The lead officer walked back out.

"You're here to look around?" he asked.

"I'm going to get married here," Ivy said.

The officer frowned. "Bad idea. We're taking you in on suspicion of conspiracy to commit murder."

"We didn't murder anyone or know anything about it. We came in that door. I never got that far," I said.

"Save it for the station. We'll get your statements," he said.

"We're not going. We're not under arrest. You can't do this." Ivy jumped up and ran for the door.

"No! Ivy!" I called.

She was tackled by an officer and cuffed.

"Now you're both under arrest," the officer said to me.

"I want my lawyer and my phone call," I replied calmly. Ivy needed a timeout but I wasn't guilty of anything except possibly trespassing

The officer nodded. "You don't look homeless. Stupid to be here but not homeless."

"And not a killer," I shot back. I bit my lip to keep myself in check.

Innocent or not, the police could make my life hell on principle or be harder on Ivy just because.

The cuffs snapped on my wrists and I wanted to freak out. I didn't like the feeling at all. I could get out of them, snap the chain with my mind—call my brother or my angels. But it wouldn't help Ivy. She was too unpredictable and I had to help her. She'd helped me so many times in the past. Whatever was messing with her head, I couldn't leave her.

ALONE IN AN INTERROGATION ROOM, I CLOSED MY EYES AND tried to reach my brother. He was asleep so he'd probably think it was just a trick or a test.

The door opened and and a guy in plainclothes walked in. "I'm Detective Harper. I know you," he said.

"Hi, yeah. I work with Matt Weathers sometimes. I think some of your officers were more arrest than talk. The situation was weird. Can you call Matt or let me make my call?" I asked.

He set my purse on the table. "Why were you there?"

"Ivy wants that building for her wedding. I know, it's

crazy, but she wanted to see it at night. That place had a lot of homeless but I never saw any body," I said.

He nodded. "Make your call. I'll text Matt for good measure. But your friend isn't cooperating. She's acting like we're the enemy. The boys might've been overzealous to cuff you and everything but they say she bolted. Are they lying?"

I shook my head. "She said she saw a body, too. If she did, she might've been in shock. Terrified."

"Yeah. Make your call," he said.

I grabbed my phone, glad I'd put it on the charger. "Can I ask? Was there a body?"

He nodded. "At the back entrance."

"She's not crazy then. Freaked out." I found Matt's number and hit it to dial. I could see the body in my mind, carved open and tossed aside.

The detective left. After I explained to Matt what happened, he was on his way. I hung up and debated my options. I didn't want to call anyone else. Summoning Death wouldn't help, either. The room had one-way mirrors and they'd all think I was nuts talking to myself.

The detective entered before I had any other bright ideas.

"Matt's on his way. Ivy is calming down. You need anything?" he asked.

"What happened to the person? Was it someone home-less?" I asked.

"Looks like it. I don't exactly know. Coroner is on the scene. There was a lot of blood. May have been a suicide gone wrong. Fight. Heck, I've heard of homeless fight clubs. Sounds like he was dumped there. We interviewed some of the squatters who stay there."

"Everyone scattered," I said.

He grinned. "True. The initial raid was a bit more aggressive, but we had an outreach team go and talk to everyone after we cleared the scene. The death didn't happen there so you're free to go once we get all the info you have."

"I don't have any. You know what I know. We walked in and saw some homeless people. Ivy went back to see the other rooms and then there was screaming. That place is haunted but that's nothing new." I shrugged.

"Yep. Not worried about charging a ghost. I am concerned about you trespassing on property that is dangerous. The homeless, they squat wherever. We found a couple of windows at the back have locks that are broken. Odds are someone slips in there and unlocks the door. That's assuming the owner goes by there and locks it when he checks up on the building. I think you need to talk your friend into another place," he said.

I checked my phone for texts. "Believe me, I've been trying. Who is the owner?"

"That's not the point. I don't think he'll charge anyone with trespassing but it's a crime scene. You don't want a wedding there. You don't want to keep going back," the detective warned.

The door opened. Matt walked in looking annoyed and dressed very casually.

"I'm sorry. You know how Ivy can get," I said.

Matt nodded. "Let's go."

"Is she okay?" I grabbed my purse.

"Greg and Brody are handling her. Bridezilla is out of control," he said.

"I know. What can I do?" I asked. "Thanks, Harper."

"Night," the detective said.

"Thanks," Matt echoed.

We walked out of the station into the fresh air. "Thanks. Sorry. She woke me out of a dead sleep and I was trying to pacify her."

"Greg dropped Gunner at the warehouse. He's going to drive Ivy's car back." Matt opened the door on his vehicle for me.

I sat on the passenger side.

"Where's Ivy?" I asked.

"She's back home already. They wanted her out of the station." Matt got behind the wheel.

"What? Wait, I had to stay longer?" I asked. "Ivy needs help."

"I agree, but once they knew you two had nothing to do with the death, they wanted her gone. I can't blame them. She was acting crazy. What are we going to do about Ivy?" Matt asked.

I leaned on the window. "I don't know. Maybe once the wedding is over, she'll settle down?"

"You're a shrink," he said. "Gunner says Ivy has been missing work and Brody is covering for her. She's obsessing over random things. Details of the wedding."

"Brides get weird. That doesn't explain why she's being drawn to very haunted places. It's not like her," I admitted.

Matt looked at me while stopped at a red light. "Is she possessed?"

"No, she's not carrying around any demons but I think she's feeling it more. She was always the grounded force. Felt nothing, saw nothing. I think that's changing and it's like a hit of adrenaline to her. The engagement party at the plantation made no sense but she insisted."

"It is like she's high," Matt agreed.

"We have to try and reduce her exposure. Crap, she's so used to the house that it takes a lot." I sighed. "Where were you tonight? I wanted to bring you along on this weird wedding chore."

"Gunner and I were out at an event," he said.

"At one in the morning?" I asked.

"It was a lock-in for LGBTQ teens. I didn't tell you. Sorry," he said.

"Don't be sorry. You don't owe me an accounting of everything you do. I just thought you guys were homebodies. Maybe I'm too reliant on you two," I wondered.

"A case is one thing. This is about a wedding. You don't need to get involved in a potential murder and arrest over a wedding. I want to help Ivy and you but Ivy isn't making it easy," he said.

"I agree there. I'm trying to get her to be reasonable." I exited the car as soon as it was parked in front of my house.

Greg met us at the door. "Ivy is in bed. Brody is handling her."

"There was a body. I didn't see it, but it must have upset her," I said.

"She's seen bodies before," Matt countered.

I nodded. "I think she's becoming sensitive. She's never been like that before. That's why she keeps picking horribly haunted places."

Greg sighed. "Maybe, but it might just be nerves. Wedding stress. She never thought she'd get to be married. She wants it done before it's illegal again."

"I can't blame her there but she's going to make herself sick," Matt said.

"Sorry, I've been trying to be a good friend. I couldn't

check her. Maybe Brody can bring her down to earth. A wedding is one day. The marriage is every day. One day can't be perfect no matter how much work you put into it," I said.

"Get some sleep. We'll talk it over in the morning," Greg said.

"Thanks." I headed upstairs.

In the quiet of my room, I wondered if it was my fault. Was my group under attack? Paul had been weird. Ivy obsessed with haunted places. Matt and Gunner sneaking off and not telling us where. Greg was cultivating new religious trainees. Only Mary Lou seemed unchanged lately.

I didn't bother to change. I crawled into bed and pulled the covers over my head. The raised voices from Ivy's room broke my heart. I should be able to help but I was too close to Ivy. She'd been my rock for years.

Her and Greg…

I wanted to be there for them but Ivy wasn't letting me. She wasn't listening.

Chapter Five

"BREAKFAST?" Frankie asked.

I groaned and looked at the clock. It was nearly nine in the morning but I'd slept like a rock after the late-night adventures.

"You're bringing me breakfast in bed? Am I sick?" I teased.

"Hunk of cornbread with a file in it." Frankie set it on the bed.

"Ha-ha." I sat up and rubbed my eyes. "Is Matt mad?"

"I think you just interrupted a fun event. Ivy is freaked about the body. Brody can't get her to come out of their room. She's acting…"

"I know." I broke off a piece of cornbread. "No coffee?"

Tish sniffed the cornbread and batted at the nail file.

"Are you going to spend the day in bed?" Frankie teased.

I shook my head. "Let me get ready. Make sure there is coffee."

"Okay. I saw a few good houses yesterday but I'm going to look at more today. Do you need anything?" he asked.

I shook my head. "Did you have any weird dreams last night?"

He smiled. "Yeah, I didn't think it was real. My sister doesn't get arrested."

"That's what I thought. I should've bugged you harder," I teased.

"I would've gone for Matt anyway." Frankie shrugged. "I'll take this down so the cat doesn't make a mess."

"Thanks." I watched my brother leave and close the door behind him.

I got up and locked the door. Grabbing my phone, I knew I had to do something to help Ivy. I had to text Paul.

Me: *Ivy is really obsessed with the wedding venue and these haunted places. I'm worried about her health. Can you make a house call?*

Paul: *Sure, I'll be there in a few minutes. Matt said you were arrested?*

Me: *Misunderstanding. Not officially arrested or booked anyway.*

Paul: *Troublemaker*

I replied with an emoji and headed for the bathroom.

By the time I was in the kitchen, Paul was there talking to my brother.

I got coffee. "Where's Ivy?" I asked.

"Still in bed. I tried," Frankie said.

"I'll go get her." I trudged back up the stairs and tapped on her door.

"Go away," Ivy called.

I tried the door. "Let me in. We have to talk."

"I saw Paul's car. I'm not sick," Ivy said.

"You are feeling things more. You're being pulled to more

haunted places. Paul knows what that feels like. Frankie, too. Why don't you talk to them? I understand you're used to haunted places and there aren't many ghost or demon-free areas around here but you're going toward places with issues and violence. That's not where you plan an event," I said.

She yanked the door open. She was still in her robe and fuzzy slippers. "I know that's the right place."

"That's why I want you to talk to Paul. I know it's not the right place. I trusted you and Greg a lot when I first moved here. You trusted my abilities. Trust me now. Take it down a notch," I said.

Ivy brushed past me to the stairs. "I'm coming down for coffee."

I smiled and watched her little dog, Pearl, scamper after Ivy.

I headed down slowly and kept quiet as I refilled my coffee.

"Ivy, have you talked to Greg about this? Getting attached to the dangerous hauntings might mean something attached to you. Marked you," Paul suggested.

"They can do that?" Frankie asked.

"If you give them an opening, they can cling to it. Some people use and harness demonic powers. But a demon has their own juice. They're fallen angels, so it's limited but it's there." I shrugged.

"I'll talk to Greg. Sounds good," Ivy agreed quickly.

I shared a look with Paul.

"Okay, well, I'll stay on the good side of things. Darla and I are out looking at properties again. See ya. Stay out of jail," Frankie said.

I nodded. "I promise."

Ivy's phone chimed. "Yes, the owner replied. He wants to meet me."

"Invite him here," Paul said.

"What?" I asked.

"Good idea, the crime scene is probably still active." Ivy texted back.

Seconds later her phone dinged again. "He's coming around noon. Perfect. I have to go get ready with my plans."

Ivy dashed upstairs, her furry friend close behind.

I grabbed a yogurt from the fridge. "Greg? That's the best you've got?"

Paul shrugged. "She's fine. She knows who she is, where she is, and all the normal stuff. You know that."

"I know but maybe she's manic. Aren't there tests you can run for bipolar?" I asked.

He shook his head. "She's not that manic. She's not so off that it might be that. People get crazy with weddings."

"I know, but she's extra. Maybe it is something she picked up from the angel bar and I never noticed. I don't feel it on her." I shrugged.

"Maybe it's just an attachment. I don't think it's all the time. She was calm just now." Paul refilled his coffee.

The doorbell rang. It was too soon for the owner of the warehouse. I went and found Eli without Greg.

"Hi," I said.

"Hello, I heard about your unfortunate incarceration. Is everything well?" he asked.

"False alarm. Greg's already gone," I said.

Eli nodded. "I understand. I wanted to convey a dream I had about the wedding."

"Everyone gets prophetic dreams now. I'll be put out of business. Come on in," I said.

"I don't know if it's true or not but the wedding inside the warehouse was deadly. Many people fell ill and died," he said.

"That's your dream?" I led the way into the kitchen.

"Father," Paul said.

"Doctor," Eli replied.

"Died?" Paul asked.

"The padre had a dream about Ivy's wedding," I filled in. "Coffee?"

"No, thank you," the priest replied. "Later, I had a dream where the wedding took place in the gardens here at the mansion and it was peaceful. If you want to take that as a sign."

"I'm more worried about Ivy right now. She's acting odd. Paul is wondering about a demonic attachment. If you and Greg can work on that, it all might work out," I said.

The priest smiled. "That is not a diagnosis I'd expect from a medical professional."

"I have unusual friends," Paul said. "It's not official, anyway. I have no way to test it. But if a demon found an opening to latch on—"

"I agree. If we go by the Bible, the mere fact that it is a gay wedding might be enough," the priest said.

"What?" Paul asked.

"I have gay people living here. I'm not getting attacked or attached," I replied.

The priest nodded. "Your efforts to not judge others and to help them by providing room and board would be in keeping with all attributes of a good Samaritan. Attacking your friends hurts you without bringing your direct wrath on the demons. I'm sure they don't want that."

"You know of my wrath?" I asked.

The priest swallowed hard. "May I get a glass of water?"

"Sure." I grabbed a glass from the cupboard and used the dispenser on the fridge to put ice and a water into the glass.

I handed it to him. "Wrath?"

He sipped the water. "Thank you. I only meant Greg has recounted a lot of stories about you. The will to fight and believe you will win against true evil—it takes tenacity."

"Whatever demon it is, they are trying to fly under the radar by going after Ivy and making her a manic bride. We'll dismiss it as normal." That actually made sense.

"But demons don't really need any opening, do they?" Greg asked.

"No, they don't need one. It gives them more power to keep attacking. More authority. If you stole money then they can steal from you, rob you in a sense. Angel intervention would be blocked. If you're going by Biblical doctrine, anyway. There are courts in Heaven." The priest sipped his water again.

"I thought once you're in, you're in," I said.

"Once you're dead and judged—yes. But the living pray for intercession all the time. All prayers are heard, but are they all granted? No. Some are blocked by bad behavior. Some are on hold. Some get a different answer than the person wanted." Eli shrugged.

"So they're going hard at Ivy over a Biblical technicality?" I asked.

"Technicality?" Eli repeated.

Paul smiled. "The Bible has been translated a lot to get it into English. Is the translation accurate? King James edition?"

"We had chicken smothered with cheese at dinner last night. Are we in trouble for not keeping kosher?" I asked.

"Christians aren't subject to Jewish rules. I can debate religion all you like. It's a great pastime I enjoy with a rabbi friend. But it doesn't change that it might be the opening the demons are exploiting. I don't know if it helps the resolution or not." Eli smiled. "I'm learning and trying to help."

"Thanks. Sometimes I just feel like I'm spinning my wheels trying to understand." I put my coffee cup in the sink and switched to water myself.

Eli nodded. "That is the best thing. Trying to do the right thing. Effort is never ignored. Our world is more complicated but God doesn't change. You two are not married?"

"No," Paul said.

Eli looked back and forth between us. "You should not live together until you are."

"Catholic school flashbacks," I muttered.

"What?" Paul asked.

"Nothing," I said louder.

"If you do things God's way from the beginning, the power and blessings are bigger," Eli said.

Where did Greg dig this guy up?

"Thanks. Can I just ask, why are you shadowing a former priest? Greg left the church," I said.

"I know." Eli gave a sympathetic head tilt. "He wanted to help more people. The bishop in New Orleans at the time, and the cardinal too, they refused many requests for help with exorcism. They wanted to write it off as a medical issue. They didn't want the liability of a priest making a mistake. We have different leaders now, more willing to help. Greg kept friends with the church leadership and they understand why he did what he did. That's why the monks work with him. His training is good and his faith is strong."

I frowned. "You don't think he'd go back and take orders again?"

Eli blinked slowly. "I have no idea. His vocation is between him and God."

"Sure, of course," Paul said.

I chuckled. "Thanks for the heads up about the dream. We'll make sure to steer Ivy toward the gardens as best we can."

Eli stood up. "Thank you for the lively chat." He shook Paul's hand and whispered something to him.

Then he moved to me, putting his glass in the sink, then shook my hand. "I won't take up more of your time. But if you need anything, I'm ready to help and learn."

"Thank you." I released his hand.

"I'll show myself out. More calls to make," he said.

Once the front door closed, I looked at Paul.

"I think he's off. Ignore him," Paul said.

"I don't know. I think demons who have access makes sense. If a kid dabbles with a Ouija board, he's opening a door. That's asking for it, in a way. It doesn't mean I won't help them." I sat across from Paul. "What did he say to you?"

"You don't know?" Paul teased.

"I think I know." I wanted another cup of coffee and not to talk about this. "Everyone is a sinner. That's human nature. I'm not going to not help someone because they opened a door or like guys over girls. I can't choose who I help so it's an interesting theory. Good to know the fight might be harder than someone who accidentally stumbles on a cursed object."

"True, free will is a fun monkey wrench," Paul said.

"You were right, we need to get Greg on this. I wonder

where he went today." I checked my phone for messages and realized it was getting a lot closer to noon than I expected.

THE DOORBELL RANG AND I HAD A BAD FEELING ABOUT WHAT was on the other side.

Then again, when had this warehouse given me a good feeling? Ivy had her plans and notes all ready. Paul had fled to work and I didn't blame him a bit. I envied him, honestly.

I answered the door. The man felt menacing in his energy but he wore a Hawaiian shirt and sandal with socks. He also had a staff like a walking stick.

"I'm looking for Ivy," he said.

"Sure, come in. I'm Deanna, one of the bridesmaids. Ivy is in here." I led the way.

"I'm Dr. Malek. I've had a very busy morning. The police found some poor unfortunate soul dead in the alley behind my warehouse." He sat down at the head of the dining room table as Ivy came down the stairs and found us.

"I know. I'm so sorry about that. But I still loved your space." Ivy gushed. "I hope we can make this work. I want to give back to the areas that are impoverished."

"Yet you live here?" Malek asked.

"It's my house, been in the family for generations. It's so big it's nice to have friends stay. Roommates," I said.

"I see. Much like you, I'm very generous and fortunate. I let the homeless shelter in my warehouse. I've been trying to sell the warehouse but when they find out people have died there, it gets tricky," he said.

"Can I get you some coffee or water?" I offered.

"No, thank you," he said.

"I can't buy it but I'd love to rent it out for a day or two.

That gives us time to decorate and we'll clean up. The homeless would be out of luck for a couple of days but it's not an official shelter," Ivy said.

Dr. Malek shook his head. "No, it's not. I looked into turning it into a shelter but the liability is too much. I don't intend for people to stay there. I keep it locked to prove I'm not encouraging squatting but they find ways in."

"How many have died in your warehouse?" I asked.

"Several over the years. I don't keep track. Most of it is natural causes. They don't have the best healthcare, a shame. Some fall trying to get in. Other times there is a disagreement, people fight. Or are attacked. I can't be there to ensure safety," he said.

He had an answer for everything.

"What do you do for a living, if you don't mind my asking," I said.

"I'm a witch doctor," he said.

Ivy leaned in. "Fascinating."

I bit my lower lip.

"What do you do, Deanna?" he asked.

"I resolve paranormal situations. Hauntings and possessions, sometimes help the police," I replied.

He smiled. "Living here you, must be well off. Perhaps you should buy the warehouse and make it a shelter. It would help me."

"But renting it out wouldn't?" I asked.

"No, I'm sorry. It's not fit for an event right now. Clean up and repairs to make it safe would cost money. That would make the fee much higher. Plus, the liability insurance for events? I don't have that in place. It's not worth the hassle," he said.

Ivy looked like her wedding was canceled.

"But it's perfect. I don't even care about the death," Ivy said.

"Dr. Malek, I need to tell you that there are demons and ghosts in your warehouse. That might be causing a lot of problems. Luring homeless people there, it could be a great place to reap souls." I had to warn him even if he was part of it. A witch doctor might be part of commanding the demonic presence. On the off chance he wasn't sure of it, I had to give him a chance.

The man was hard to read. I got his energy but not his intent. I hated the sensation. He was blocking me.

The man nodded. "I'm sure there are things there no one can explain. I'd love to sell it. But until then, I just leave it empty. Probably best for the winter. The shelters get over-crowded and that makes things worse. If people choose to use that space for temporary shelter, I'm glad it's there. Now, if you don't mind, I have my own work."

"What exactly is that work? As a witch doctor, shouldn't you be able to make that space safe?"

"I'm more of a faith healer, but I don't discriminate. Everyone is welcome to access my services." He handed me a card.

"No, you can't leave. This is where my wedding is meant to be," Ivy insisted.

I texted Greg as I walked the witch doctor out of my home. I needed my house blessed and cleansed of this guy's negative energy and Ivy needed her cousin's help.

"De!" Ivy burst into tears as soon as I closed the front door.

I hugged her. "I think the gardens would be safer. I don't trust him."

She pulled away and ran up the stairs.

Chapter Six

IVY REFUSED to come out of her room the next day. Brody texted me that Greg and Mary Lou were on the way and that I should probably get out of the house for a bit.

I knocked on Matt's door and he opened it, dressed and ready for work.

"Hi, I need to find out about the people who've died in that warehouse," I said.

He nodded. "I figured. Let's grab some breakfast out and talk."

We went to a favorite place and sat outside on the patio.

"How's Paul?" Matt asked.

I frowned. "Okay. I think he's taking on too much work and I'm too sucked into the wedding. The rehabs were a great idea but I need to hire more people to run them. He's getting too involved."

Matt tilted his head. "He's choosing to get involved. Not-for-profit doesn't mean everyone works for free. Hire people with your vision."

"Don't talk about visions, please," I said as I rubbed my forehead.

"Sorry. I just worry about you and I think Paul is good for you, but you and he need to be reasonable about what you can do. This stuff takes energy and time. Even helping Ivy gets you into a case that you never saw coming," Matt said.

He'd gone for fruit and healthier options. I thought my eggs and bacon were healthy enough.

"That's my life. How's Gunner? He's been busy lately. I mean, no case so no pressure but he's always off somewhere," I said.

Matt nodded. "Mary Lou asked him to help a bit. Teach the girls in the program she runs self-defense. Being gay, there are no issues with demonstrations or working with them physically. She doesn't want them being triggered. Some of those girls were very abused but knowing Gunner has a boyfriend and all that seems to diffuse the fear of being up-close with a man for most of them."

"Learning how to kick a man into submission probably helps, too," I teased.

"Absolutely. Then the new priest Greg has been hanging with asked Gunner to show him around the city a bit. He's an odd fellow," Matt said.

"Eli, yeah. I had a weird visit from him. I guess it's good for Greg to stay current but Eli is a little eager. I really wanted to talk about the warehouse. Did you find the killer?" I asked.

Matt shook his head. "It was ruled natural causes."

"Natural? Someone dumped the body," I replied a bit too loudly, my agitation obvious.

Matt looked around. "Maybe we should wait for the station."

"No, sorry. I heard tires screeching, stop and then take off again. Then Ivy found a body." I chewed a piece of bacon while trying to get any read on the dead man.

"They did an autopsy. Heart attack. No sign of anything but some injections, probably a drug user. The tox screen didn't show poison. Odds are he was crashing with drug-using friends. He died of a heart attack and they freaked. Dumped him in an alley. It happens a lot. They don't want the police in that drug house and bodies start to smell so they get someone with a car and move the body." Matt shrugged.

"That's so sad." I lost my appetite.

"It is but not a real crime. I mean, not one we can really go after. It benefits no one. There have been some suspicious deaths on the property but most are homeless related. Not a shock. Some fights, and more overdoses. A few people were reported missing by homeless that were interviewed but they could've just moved to another place." Matt signaled for the check.

I finished my coffee. "I get that part, but what if something happened to them?"

"Unless they land in the morgue, we won't know. Some move to another warm city and some find a new group to hang out with. You can't obsess over this or it'll make you nuts. The only really unsolved cases involve a few younger homeless people. They had needle marks in the arm. A lot of stab wounds. It was chalked up to a homeless fight club." Matt stopped talking as the server brought the check.

I smiled and tried to grab it.

"I've got it," Matt said.

"Matt, don't be the old-fashioned guy." I didn't need to pay every time, but I didn't expect men to always pick up the check, either.

"I live in your house with my boyfriend. It helps my guilt," Matt said.

I shook my head. "No guilt. I need Gunner for my work. Neither you nor I need a big mansion to ourselves. But I get it's weird. We're all too old for roommates but the house is huge."

Matt smiled. "We've been thinking of moving to a little place of our own."

I nodded. "I get it. Frankie is, too."

"Ivy and Brody?" Matt asked.

"Ivy is acting so weird I don't know if she needs her own space or to be stuck in a convent for a while," I confessed.

Matt laughed so hard the little round table shook. "That's a picture."

"Greg is with her now. I don't know if it's hyper bride mania or demon attachment or more powers or a combination of the above. She's not talking to me. Ivy never doesn't talk to me."

"We're all going through changes. Brody is the main person in her life, I get that but I hope Greg can help her. It's a wedding, something will go wrong. It's life. But having it at a nice hall with a staff would minimize problems. She wants to save money but it's a wedding." I sighed, relieved to have unloaded all that.

He paid for breakfast. "Want to come to the station and look at any of the files?"

I shook my head. "No, I should research the owner more. He gives me the creeps."

"You research?" Matt asked.

I shrugged. "You just convinced me this isn't really a case. Accidental deaths and a fight club. All that says is we need another homeless shelter."

Matt frowned like he didn't believe me.

Damn! He knew me too well. I wasn't convinced but whatever was going on, I felt the witch doctor had more to do with things and it wasn't personal. He was allowing the homeless to squat for a reason. He was letting demons and ghosts hang there as well.

"Want a ride home?" he offered.

"I'm going to text Paul and we can research together, hopefully," I said.

"Good idea." Matt waved as he left.

I texted Paul and hoped he'd be up for it. We needed time together. I hated when we weren't in sync.

"DR. MALEK, A WITCH DOCTOR?" PAUL WAS ON HIS LAPTOP IN the office of the rehab. I sat next to him as he searched.

"Ivy really isn't letting up?" Paul asked.

I shook my head. "I don't get it. It feels like a case but nothing I've done before. The place has demons and ghosts, yes. The owner is a bit freaky. But I don't feel like Ivy is possessed. I can't sort out the supernatural problem at the core. I'm spinning my wheels and supposed to be doing wedding stuff."

Paul smiled.

"What?"

"You don't want a big fancy wedding?" he asked.

I shrugged and paced the room to avoid too much direct eye contact. "I've done the bridesmaids thing plenty.

Standing up with drag queens, that's a bit intimidating but I just want Ivy to have a good day. It'll never be perfect."

"I asked about you," Paul said.

I tilted my head as my neck tensed. "I know. I don't know. Some girls have planned their wedding since preschool. I never really did. I mean, who knows who the guy would be? Maybe he wants something specific?"

"Guys don't care about dresses and flowers," Paul said.

"Do I? Other than my dress, really?" I asked.

"Your mother was very OCD, I'm guessing," he said.

"She is. Controlling too, why?" I sat back down.

Paul nodded. "She controlled things. Her way meant peace, your way meant conflict. Here you get your way. But a wedding means family and mother of the bride stuff. If you don't decide, you can let her plan and have peace."

"You're such a shrink," I said.

"You are, too. It's just hard to get our patterns from childhood totally out of us. No matter how well adjusted we are, there's always something." He leaned over and kissed me.

I felt a million pounds lighter. "Thanks. Ivy changed out the dresses to red. Like a crazy bold red with a slit up to my hip."

He smiled. "You'll look amazing. Heels?"

"It's Ivy, of course," I replied.

He chuckled. "One day. For our wedding, I don't care if you wear flats or sneakers."

I wanted to laugh or ask a question but I just froze.

Paul didn't save me and say anything, either.

Finally, I recovered just enough. "Want some water? I'm going to grab one from the fridge."

"I'm fine," he said.

I walked slowly to the office fridge and got a bottle of water. Walking back even slower, I reviewed what he said. It wasn't a proposal. There was no ring or question.

As I reached for the door handle, I suddenly regretted the water. What if he was in there on one knee holding a ring?

Checking myself, I hadn't felt any of this coming. Either he covered really well or it wasn't a proposal and I was freaking out for nothing.

I opened the door and he was safely in his chair. I breathed a bit easier.

"Anything on the witch doc?" I asked.

"Really, nothing about what I said?" He answered my question with a question.

"Flats are fine." I opened the water and sipped it.

Paul shook his head but at least he was smiling.

"What? I'm not stepping on Ivy's wedding. I'm shocked Matt and Gunner haven't run off to Vegas or something," I said.

"So there is an order to who can get engaged and married when? Your mom has the OCD?" he teased.

I smacked his shoulder. "We have a case."

"We have a weird guy. He's actually a doctor, sort of. Chiropractor. Not poor. Plenty of investments. The warehouse is probably an investment property. That's down in the lower Ninth Ward. He probably got it for a song after Katrina and wants to flip it for a profit." Paul shrugged. "Probably did some dark magic stuff too to drag in spirits or whatever. He's not going to keep it so might as well sell something haunted. He could turn it into a big attraction if he wanted."

I nodded. "You're right. Any criminal history?"

"You just had breakfast with Matt," Paul said.

"Right, I'll ask him. Anything with the medical boards, reprimands or anything weird?" I asked.

"Um, he also has a mortician's license, oddly. That's not usually something you do and not practice," Paul said.

"Weird to combine that with being a chiropractor." I hummed to myself for a bit. "Why do you think Matt and Gunner haven't made it official?"

"Ask them. Not everyone does or wants to." He looked me dead in the eye.

"Are you tying to use that creepy warning from Eli to get me to commit?" I teased.

Paul rolled his eyes. "I think we're committed. Our lives are complicated. It'd be better if we were together more."

"We should hire someone else to spearhead the rehabs. Someone who believes what we do but can make overseeing the clinics," I suggested.

He nodded. "That's a start."

"I don't want to do anything because a weird priest said something," I protested.

"We don't have to do anything, but neither of us are so weak that we'd do it because of a weird new guy," Paul replied.

I sighed and looked up mortician legalities on my phone. "I know. You moving in would be good but my mother and father would…Frankie might even be weird about it but he's looking for his own house."

"That's not the priest getting in your head?"

I sat up straight. "No, that's parents. And I don't want to jinx it. Some things like giving the bride away are dumb. I'm not property. But moving in before you're committed? It's like that old saying about milk for free. Only this is free rent and food."

"Like I wouldn't pay my way," Paul scoffed.

"I know and I know my friends live there for free. It's just this is different. I don't want to screw it up. That's why I think I let work pull me away sometimes. My life gets to be too much for you but I'm used to it." I leaned my head on his shoulder.

"I can handle more than you think." He kissed the top of my head.

"I know. Let's just get through Ivy's wedding then we can talk more about things," I suggested.

"Okay. I think you might have a case after all," he said.

"Why?" I asked.

Paul pointed to the laptop screen. "The warehouse has had upgrades and there was work done on the roof after Hurricane Katrina. It's not condemned. It's had two recent inspections from near sales. The value is good. He shouldn't have a problem selling it if he wants to."

"Maybe he got close and changed his mind, wanted to sit on it for a bit and make more? If it's an investment," I replied.

"Maybe." Paul sent a link to the info to my email. "Who do you know that might help with real estate questions?"

I smiled. "Can't hurt to ask."

FRANKIE HAD BEEN TEXTING ME PICTURES ALL DAY. IT WAS nice he'd found something that excited him. The variety of architecture around New Orleans was crazy. It just wasn't my thing.

However, once Frankie said that he wanted me to come

and see a place he was seriously considering, I'd texted him to bring Darla over for dinner so we could talk about the prospects first.

"You're cooking?" Gunner sniffed the air as he entered the kitchen.

"I'm not that bad," I said.

"I'm helping." The houseboy came in from the dining room. "Spicy shrimp and blackened chicken with potatoes and rice and beans. Cornbread?"

"No, rolls," I vetoed. Cornbread was lovely but it didn't go with everything.

"Biscuits." The houseboy went to work.

I rolled my eyes.

"What's all this about? We're not moving out tomorrow," Gunner said softly.

I frowned. "What? I like having you here."

"I liked being here but it seems like that isn't necessary anymore." Gunner looked around.

"Is it Ivy? Greg is working with her. I think it's the wedding stuff and maybe she's getting more sensitive. Nothing super dangerous," I said.

Gunner shook his head. "It's not her. Matt was grieving his mother. His brother moved. He needed to be surrounded by friends. Now, it's more like we're guests here and we want our privacy in our own place."

"Who isn't giving you privacy?" I asked.

Chuckling, Gunner hugged me. "It's not that. It's your house. We want our space."

"Are you engaged?" I asked.

Gunner blushed. "No, relax. I know Frankie is looking. We're not leaving for a reason other than we're ready."

"You're sure it's not because of Paul? He's not pushing to

move in and I'm not dragging him in." I checked the potatoes.

"It's not him. He's good for you. He loves you. He's a good guy. People don't stay in the same place all their life. It's good to move on. Ivy and Brody might need their own space eventually." Gunner sampled a potato. "Mmmm."

"Thanks. The trick is lots of butter." I turned down the heat. "Oh God, if the place empties out Greg will fill it with priests or former nuns or something."

"Now he needs to move out," Gunner said. "I like the guy but he's floating between here and Mary Lou and the church. The guy is in limbo and he's working like crazy to avoid his life."

"Crap, you're right. How did I not see that?" I asked.

"You're too close. Having a team for your work is wonderful but you need a life. You need distance from your team so you can see if they are off their game. He's good at what he does but he's losing himself in the fight. He needs a life too. Monastic or married—something." Gunner checked the chicken. "I think it's done."

"Thanks." I took it out and cut into a piece. "Looks good."

The doorbell rang.

"Damn it," I said.

"I'll get this. Go answer the door. Paul coming too?" Gunner teased.

"I cooked for an army. Everyone is invited," I said.

I wanted to see everyone but Darla was the one I needed to get on the case. Hopefully, she didn't mind using her real estate connections for good without profit.

"YOU MADE THIS?" PAUL ASKED AFTER HE'D SAMPLED THE chicken.

"With help, yes." I smiled. "I figured if a priest can use it —all the demons must be gone."

"Demons were in your kitchen?" Eli asked.

Greg had brought Eli along.

"No, just a ghost. But I would get distracted by cases and people and let things burn. I'm not a terrible cook but other things always trumped it. Thought I'd give it a shot again," I said.

"I'm so flattered to be invited to a family dinner. I know you'll love some of these cute little homes. It's so hard to pick," Darla said.

"Flipping or living?" I asked.

"I'll start small. Buy one at a time and rehab. Assess with a contractor, do what I can and hire people for the rest. I'll know the right house for me when I find it," Frankie replied.

"Time would be a factor to make a profit," I said.

Darla nodded. "Career flippers would buy and turn them over in weeks. But that means a big bill and the risk that someone might not pay what you did, plus what you put into it, plus profit."

"I should have time tomorrow to go see a few of them," I said.

"Might I join you? I'd love to feel out a home. Are they haunted?" Eli asked.

I shared a look with Paul. He grinned.

"I'm going to the bank tomorrow," Ivy said.

Brody sighed.

"What for?" I asked.

"I need a loan. I'm going to buy the warehouse," she said.

Greg put down his knife and fork. "Ivy, we talked about this. You don't need it. You don't want to use it for a business. You're not going to buy it just for one day."

"It's my wedding, I need it," Ivy seethed.

"Why?" Paul asked.

Ivy glared at him like he'd mocked her.

"Ivy, we're just trying to understand," I jumped in.

Ivy took a deep breath. "I don't expect you to understand. You've neve been married. You're not even engaged. It's my day. *The day!*"

Mary Lou took the hint. "I have been married. I understand you want a great party and a perfect day but you can't control everything with so little time. You need to remember it is Brody's wedding, too. It'll be fabulous no matter where it is. Don't stress yourself out over one piece."

"I knew this was a mistake." Ivy stomped away from the table.

Brody and Greg chased her but I was done babying her.

"I'm sorry," I said to Darla.

She smiled. "I deal with it all the time. Buying a house is very stressful, too. Moving and financing. Couples often have huge fights."

"Do you deal with any commercial or investment properties like warehouses?" I asked.

"No, I deal with residential but I have friends who do. What do you need?" he asked.

"I just want to figure out this warehouse she's obsessed with. History of ownership. Sales. The guy who owns it now claims to be a witch doctor and that he wants to sell but Paul looked it up and seems like he's had plenty of offers. Can you check it out and let me know?" I asked.

"De," Frankie warned.

"What? This might not be a paranormal problem. Someone died but it seems like natural causes from the autopsy. Some people have died there but if it's full of homeless people and some are addicts, so the odds are some will overdose or die of neglected health issues. Maybe it's not always the demon?" I asked.

"That would be very dull," Eli said.

I looked at him. "If you enjoy the demonic, you're in the wrong business and will be doing their bidding in a few months," I warned him.

Eli's smile faded. "I'm only trying to gain firsthand experience. Study and theory are good but it's tedious. They test you. I'm eager to help people, not just prove my loyalty to God and innocent people."

"It's not an adrenaline rush, it's an endurance test," I explained. "You need to pace yourself, Father. Now I didn't make dessert, but we have ice cream."

Chapter Seven

STEPPING OUT OF THE SHOWER, I heard some loud voices downstairs. Quickly dressing, I ran down and found Brody, Ivy, Greg, and Mary Lou happily talking about chairs and tables.

"What's going on?" I asked.

"I'm going with the garden. I tried one last time to get the guy to rent me the warehouse and he said no. I won't let it ruin me," she said.

"Great. You seemed to have turned the corner." I didn't really buy it, but Ivy was trying. "Let me know if you need anything. I'm doing the house thing with Frankie. Greg, can I ask you something about Eli before he gets here?"

"Sure." Greg didn't move.

I nodded for him to follow me. I went into the main parlor and sat on the couch.

Greg walked in. "What's wrong?"

"I know this guy is fresh from training and Vatican City, no less, but he said something concerning. I don't want him to upset my friends." I rubbed my forehead.

It was the clash of religion and not judging people that made my head hurt. Follow these rules because they are right but…you don't get to judge others by those rules. That was just a big black hole that humans kept falling into.

"I know he's conservative," Greg said.

"He said maybe Ivy's reaction or demonic attachment or whatever is because it's a gay wedding. I don't want him at the wedding," I said.

"He's not likely to be invited," Greg said.

"He's like your shadow. He also made comments about Paul and I not living together before marriage. None of it shocks me but he's just in everyone's business. Usually you ask the priest before you get advice or absolution," I said.

Greg nodded. "I'll talk to him. They emphasize strength and purity to deal with the demonic. You have to be clean so you can truly fight and banish them. Like you said last night, he's overeager."

"Thanks. Are you okay?" I asked.

He shrugged. "Sure."

"Okay." I smiled. "I'm going to finish getting ready. I was worried when things got loud."

"Why?" he asked.

"Ivy's been nuts lately," I said.

"No, why did you ask if I'm okay?" Greg explained.

I sighed. "You've been the rock. Everyone seems to be changing, moving, planning, or spinning. You're spreading yourself thin between me, the church, and Mary Lou. You can't serve two masters. I know we serve the same boss but you can't have a relationship halfway."

"She's mad?" Greg whispered.

"She hasn't said a word but she was married to a jerk for years. You're better than he was. But you two had an affair. I don't know what's blocking you but you're not moving forward with her. I'm not sure why."

"Because I'd have to give up some of this," he confessed.

"Some. You have to choose your life. The church isn't going to tell you what to do anymore."

"You could tell me which way to go," he joked.

"No, we're too close. It'd be skewed with my feelings. You know, you'll always be my friend and I'll always need some priest and exorcist skills on my team. I'm just saying don't put your life on hold for my work. It'll never end."

"You're not putting your life on hold?" he asked.

"Not anymore. I'm not moving super-fast but I nearly have everything the way I want it. Fine tuning." I winked and headed back upstairs.

FIVE HOUSES LATER, I WAS GRATEFUL FOR WHOEVER texted me.

Until I looked at it.

Eli had my number and wanted to know if I wanted to help him with a little project. That priest was odd but something about this message felt serious. I needed to go and be sure. Trusting my gut, I decided to take the out.

It wasn't just that I wanted to get away from the house visits. Most had some ghosts. Nothing extreme, but Frankie and Darla were enjoying it a lot more than I was.

"Everything okay?" Frankie asked.

"Yeah, I just need to consult on something. People get in over their heads fast. Do you mind? I think you guys know way more about this than I do. I inherited the mansion." I shrugged.

"It's so lovely there," Darla said.

"Thanks. I couldn't imagine living there when I first came but now I can't imagine living anywhere else," I admitted. "Frankie, I know you want to go slow but if you work out one and want to do this more—I want you to have your share of Gran's money. It's only fair."

"De, I'm fine. I just don't want to live in a mansion. It's not me," he said.

I nodded. "We'll talk about it more later. Once you've gone through one of these flips. But if you need cash to buy one, let me know. I'm better than a bank."

"Thanks, bye," he said.

I drove over to the address the priest texted.

I walked up and Eli met me at the door.

"Thank you for coming." He stood a bit too close.

I backed up. Something was off with the priest, more than normal. "Is Greg here?" I asked.

"No, he was helping his cousin," Eli answered.

I frowned. "Did he talk to you?"

Eli nodded. "I realize I may have overstepped. You don't revere priests."

"I don't put them on a pedestal, no. I respect the work of good ones. I acknowledge the devotion, giving up parts of your life. I do prefer exorcists that have taken orders. What is this project?" I asked.

"It's a support group for people who've dealt with demonic attachments and possession. Like the support groups in your rehab facility. One of the women has been afflicted or feeling that she is under attack," he said.

I looked over the house. They all looked alike at this point, but I did sense evil. "Is it her home?"

Eli nodded.

"Why would you do that?" I asked.

"They rotate the meeting place. Keeping their presence united hopefully will show the demons they are being fought," Eli said.

"You're showing the demons they're still in charge. I'd have it at a church. Holy ground," I said.

"These are women who feel the church didn't help them," he said.

I frowned. "Who helped them?"

"Greg. He's been rogue for many years but effective." Eli turned to go inside.

"What do you want me along for?" I asked.

"I told you that one woman is struggling. You can help," he said.

"Greg can't?" I asked. "All those monks?"

Eli nodded. "If you don't want to help, it's fine. I thought maybe you'd like to test if you have another gift. You don't talk enough to be a prophet but healing is a big gift. Anyone can lay hands, but your results speak for themselves."

"Stop, I don't need an ego boost. That doesn't do it for me," I said.

"Humility is important in this as well."

"I've participated in exorcisms before. It's not new." I felt like this guy was wasting my time.

"I'm not asking for your help. You will cast out the demon. Alone. Prove your gift. Prove it's not just those anointed by the church," Eli challenged.

"Prove it to who? You?" I wasn't taking the bait.

I turned and walked away. As I reached my car, I heard an eerie demonic voice come from Eli.

"Coward hiding behind priests," Eli called.

The demon was in him. Some possessions weren't

permanent. Attachments allowed the demon to come and go so it was harder to verify and evict them.

"Maybe it's not my gift or my job. God and Greg can free you." I reached for the car door.

It wasn't locked but the door wouldn't open.

"Face me, witch," Eli hissed. He had followed me to the curb.

"I'm not a witch." I grabbed the spray bottle of Holy Water from my purse and turned on him—spraying liberally.

"No!" He retreated into the house.

I knew better than to go in there.

Then I heard the women shrieking.

It could be a trick but could I really take that chance?

It was a trap but I charged in. The women hid in the kitchen.

"Amy, I could use some backup," I said.

My angel appeared and the trio of angels from my home showed up in a flurry of mist.

"Start praying. How's your Latin?" Eli mocked.

My approach wasn't traditional. I walked toward him and reached out one hand. Snatching the large crucifix from the priest's neck, I turned it and pressed it to his chest. My other hand reached toward the priest. I felt the demon and mentally pulled.

My left hand was filled with evil and my right hand felt lighter.

I flung the demon to the angels without looking directly at it.

The angels did whatever they do with those fallen evil monsters. As soon as they were gone and only Amy remained, I could breathe again.

"You're free. Don't let your ego get in the way of your calling again or I'll have to summon Death to take you."

Eli was on his knees and shaking, so weak from the ordeal.

"That was fast," he cried.

"Painful too, I'm sure. If you wanted to kill me, you failed," I said.

Eli collapsed on the floor. "I needed help."

"Without backup? You hate me. You think men with collars are the only one who should do things like this. I proved you wrong. That demon played on your ego and you failed to stay pure. You failed your church. Don't come near my home again. Don't go near my brother or Greg ever again. Now get out of this woman's house before you infect it more," I commanded.

He crawled to the door.

I had no sympathy for the weak man. I took a picture of him and sent it to Greg with a text.

Me: *Your friend was possessed. You need to stick to the monks.*

I walked past him and got in my car, which was no longer demonically locked against me.

Before I started the car, I got a text. It wasn't Greg's reply. It was the ER, Paul had been hurt.

"Damn!" It was one of *those* days.

I RUSHED INTO THE ER, TRYING TO CONVINCE MYSELF THAT this was not a punishment for my casting out a demon and being so scolding. I took no credit. Without the angels I'd probably have fled.

Having the women there in danger forced my hand. I

couldn't leave or wait for Greg to arrive with the demon so intent on me and innocents nearby.

The staff at the front desk let me by without a word. It was odd but I'd been there enough with Paul, though he was normally the doctor and I was the patient.

I found him without directions. That was an old gift. He had scratches on his neck and an ice pack on his head.

"What happened?" I asked. "Dumb question. Who?"

He shook his head. "A former patient at the rehab. She went back to the ex and he got her hooked again. I knew she'd be an issue. Once she stopped the drugs, she thought that was all she had to change."

I took his free hand. "Is it just your face?"

"Minor concussion. We scanned him. Nothing is broken. The woman was arrested. Sorry, I'm Dr. Prescott," the man in a white coat entering data into a computer next to Paul's gurney said.

I shook his hand. "Thanks, nice to meet you. I'm the girlfriend."

Paul chuckled. "Ow."

"What's so funny?" I asked.

"Girlfriend?" he teased.

"Shut up. I spent the morning looking at little houses, then yanked a demon out of a priest. You're not the biggest story today." I wanted to kiss him. "Broken teeth or anything?"

"No, she was more of a tackle and scratch type. He hit his head on the ground," Dr. Prescott explained.

I nodded and leaned over, kissing Paul gently. "Was she pretty?"

"Ha," Paul said.

"He needs to be watched for a day or so but he knows

the drill. Just don't leave him alone. If he refuses to eat, gets dizzy, throws up, or his pupils stay dilated for too long, get him back here ASAP. I'll get him discharged." The doc nodded.

"Thanks," I said.

"I'm fine," Paul insisted.

"You don't want to stay over?" I teased.

"Not allowed to do anything fun until my head is cleared."

I looked at him. "I'm sorry."

"Why? It's not your fault," he said.

"It is. I was distracted by the demonic priest thing or I'd have sensed this," I said.

Paul leaned closer. "Just tell me it wasn't Greg."

I laughed. "No, the new weird one. He wasn't fully possessed but he dabbled in the power of the fallen angels and I didn't pick up on that fully. I trusted Greg's judgement. I'm slipping."

"You're helping your brother and trying to help Ivy. Stop being so hard on yourself." Paul pulled my hand to his mouth and kissed it. "Maybe we should just get married?"

"Okay, that's the concussion talking. No proposing until you've been mentally clear for at least forty-eight hours." I couldn't handle that. Not today!

Chapter Eight

OVER PIZZA, I explained the details of my day to Greg.

"You threatened him and told him to stay away?" Greg asked.

"Yes, Eli is supposed to help people and he let himself be taken over. He could've killed you or me. Those women at the support group were just playthings for that demon," I said.

Paul frowned. "You want to blame the woman who attacked me for relapsing?"

"She's an adult who is responsible for her actions. Relapse is one thing, attacking someone is next level. Yes, I'm tired of coddling people. They're adults. Stuff happens and it's good to help others but this is crazy," I said.

"You had to kick a few demons off of me once." Paul finished the pizza and grabbed some ice cream from the freezer.

"You were getting used to me. My life is weird," I defended him.

Greg sighed. "Eli is eager. He's excited and clearly let his guard down. I'll handle it. He shouldn't have called you in but cutting him off is not the right move."

I frowned. "That support group should be at a church hall, not a private home."

"Agreed but some of the women have been bothered or hurt by church situations," Greg said.

"Then a community center meeting room. Something neutral that you can bless and clean. I don't want Eli in this house," I said.

Paul handed me a spoon and shared his ice cream. "You're still on adrenaline. It'll look better tomorrow."

"You saved people, it was good. Without backup. You're on guard and hyper. I'm shocked you're not exhausted." Greg studied me.

"You think the demon jumped into me?" I asked.

Greg pulled a small tin from his pocket and opened it. He prayed in Latin as he put an oil cross on my forehead.

"Anything?" Paul asked.

I shrugged. "I feel fine. I think I've been on guard since Eli because there's a demon loose. But I know he wasn't possessed when he was at my dining table. I just don't want to make the mistakes he did."

Greg smiled. "Good. When you think you're safe, you're vulnerable. However, your guard being up is making you a bit critical."

Paul's face said he agreed.

I grumbled. "I thought I'd get a little break. Ivy's wedding was a good excuse not to jump on a case right now and nothing came up. Except a possessed priest and Ivy acting nuts about a warehouse."

Paul smiled. "Your own sort of withdrawal."

"Ha. I thought I was getting a mini vacation from stuff

and it found me. I don't get a break and I'm off my game. Eli needs help, not me making it worse." I should know better by now.

"He endangered people you care about. It's okay to be protective. You're not responsible for everyone on the planet," Paul pointed out.

"I knew there was a reason I keep you around." I kissed him.

While I was up close, I checked his pupils.

"What?" he asked.

"Any symptoms from the concussion?" I asked.

"No, I'm okay. Just gotta find a good show to binge and make some coffee since I have to stay up a while." He shrugged.

"Nothing scary. I want happy and not haunted," I said.

"I'll go check on Eli. Ivy and Brody are out doing sampling some caterers. Why they wanted a quick wedding is beyond me," Greg said.

"But Ivy is doing better?" I asked.

Greg nodded. "More or less. It's all stressful. I told her not to put that much pressure on herself but it's the big day."

"Eloping is so bad why?" I asked.

The men laughed.

"Have a good night," Greg said.

"De, wake up. De!" Paul shook my arm.

I sat up straight on the couch. "Sorry," I said.

"Don't be. You dozed off. I'm fine with coffee and TV but you were dreaming something ugly," he said.

I closed my eyes and went back to the vision. I knew it wasn't just a dream because I could recall it clearly. A group of men had entered the warehouse and kidnapped some of the homeless that were squatting there. Most of the people fled, a couple were already dead.

"I have to talk to Matt." I kissed Paul on the cheek and went for my purse and keys.

THE BODIES WERE REAL. A FEW PEOPLE HAD CALLED THE police. There were two bodies but three more were missing. The old blind woman was among the witnesses. By the time I'd caught up with Matt he was already headed for the warehouse, so I joined him there.

"What happened?" I asked the old woman.

"Someone scored drugs and was sharing. That's always a warning sign but some dealers want to get people hooked. Free samples." She shook her head. "Most of us were smart enough to say no. We tried to kick them out," she said.

"And then?" Matt asked.

She shrugged. "A couple of them fought. The people who'd tried the drugs started drifting off. Passing out. It happens. I didn't freak out. One started to convulse. I don't know who."

"You didn't call for an ambulance?" Matt asked.

"I'm blind, homeless, and old. No one believes me. Someone who saw what was happening might've," she replied.

"When did these men come in and take people?" Matt asked.

"Not long after. They took out everyone who'd passed out or was ill. But they left two. People were screaming. Most everyone ran. I hid in the back," she said.

"How do you know they left two?" I asked.

"People checked them. The two left behind were dead. Cold to the touch dead so I'm not sure that was the drugs. I'm not the best witness."

"You are the calmest," Matt said.

A couple people were still hysterical over missing friends or family members. Matt had interviewed them as best as he could.

"Thank you, we'll find a shelter for you tonight. We might need more info and we need to be able to find you," Matt said.

"People steal my stuff in shelters. I'm blind," she said.

"You trust the people in here?" I asked.

She held up her cane. "They don't kick me out for hitting thieves with my cane."

"We'll see what we can do. Mary Lou might have room," Matt suggested.

I nodded. "Good idea. Why would someone kidnap drugged homeless people?"

"Sex trafficking is a big thing," Matt said.

"Dr. Malek needs to sell this place so it can be better secured. It's not right for people to be exploited." I looked around.

"That man. The owner? He's in on it," the blind woman whispered.

"That's not how he made it sound," I replied.

She grunted. "I'm sure. He's around but sneaky. Tells people he can heal them. Lures them into vans and we never see them again."

"No offense, but how would you know?" Matt asked.

"People tell me what happens. I know what I know. I know his voice," she shot back.

"I'm taking her to Mary Lou's. We need her close," I said.

"I can feel his energy without even hearing him," she added.

"I believe you. I'd let you stay with me but my house is way too haunted," I explained.

She nodded. "Not the best place for a blind woman. Some things like to taunt and tease."

"I'm going to walk the room," I said.

Matt nodded.

I paced aimlessly trying to feel out the demons and the tricks. I touched the walls and tried to feel where the people had been taken.

The result wasn't a blank but like a brick wall. A big mental block.

Whatever this was, a case had found me despite me insisting that it hadn't.

I watched Matt interview Dr. Malek from behind glass so he couldn't see me. The witch doctor was cool in the face of kidnappings and dead bodies on his property.

"Perhaps I should just donate the warehouse to the city. Someone is liable to sue me," he said.

Matt scoffed. "That's your biggest concern? People are dead. How often do you visit this property?"

"Rarely. I've been trying to sell it," he said.

"We've had other people tell us you are there frequently," Matt countered.

Malek laughed. "They'd hide if I showed up. People walk in and the squatters flee like rats."

"You don't care?" Matt asked.

"I lock the place up, they find ways in. I'm glad they have shelter from the elements when needed. You'd rather I kept them out? I can't afford a fancy security system to monitor it all. I'd like to sell but I'm not going to take a loss," the man replied.

"We'll be checking up on your whereabouts and any activity you might have. Looking into the property history as well," Matt said.

"Am I free to go?" Malek asked.

Matt nodded. "The warehouse is a crime scene until further notice so don't try to access it. We'll be guarding it for now."

"Suit yourself. I wish there were no problems. It's a waste of a lot of time. A bad batch of drugs or a fight and people die. I'm not unfeeling but it's no one I know. I didn't hurt them." Malek stood.

Rubbing my forehead, I went out of the room and met the witch doctor in the hallway.

"Dr. Oscar. Fancy seeing you here," Malek said.

"Nice to see you again. I'm just trying to help." I reached out my hand.

He shook it and pulled his hand back fast.

I smiled and walked away.

Malek had blocked me before. I wasn't sure how or to what extent, but he'd dulled some of my powers to do with his property. The oil Greg had used on my forehead had enough pure power to counter the witch doctor

Matt caught up with me in the parking lot. "De," he said.

"That guy is up to something," I said.

Matt nodded. "Stay out of it for now. Get some sleep. You were up all night with Paul. Maybe you'll catch a vision. Odds are the people are on the move. Traffickers try to get them across state lines as soon as possible. That's my main focus now. If you get a lead, call me. You track better than most, but you'd tell me if you felt anything."

"I know. That's why I needed to confront Malek. He'd blocked me a bit. Not sure how but I'll try to help." I checked my phone. "Damn, I have a dress fitting for the wedding this morning. I'll grab a nap afterward and be a lot clearer. Sorry," I said.

"We're all doing our best." Matt patted my shoulder.

In the car, I pulled my little bottle of Holy Water from my purse. It was empty. I'd used it up on Eli. I should have refilled it immediately.

I headed home to shower and change for the wedding mania. The full crazy and then some was back.

Free to sleep, Paul was tucked in with Tish snuggled into his shoulder and purring. I'd doubled up on the under-eye concealer and looked my best as I headed off to the dress fitting.

I didn't expect Ivy to be there, but she had accompanied another bridesmaid.

It was a shop that catered to queens and others. I felt skinny and simple compared to some of the clients.

"De, I'm so glad you're here. Paul said you ran off in the middle of the night. I know cases come first," Ivy rambled.

I hugged her. "No way, your wedding is a huge deal. I wouldn't screw it up. I think you're really smart to avoid that warehouse. More people turned up dead there. I think that witch doctor is part of it. Matt's looking at angles. Some people may have been kidnapped."

"May have?" Ivy asked.

I nodded. "They were. We have witnesses but they're

homeless. I don't know if they'll want to give formal state-ments or stay put to testify."

"I'm so selfish. I'm driving everyone crazy about my wedding and people are missing," Ivy said.

"No, you can't do that. It's your day. I wouldn't know about the warehouse without you. My vision took us there faster than a 911 call. The people squatting there worry about being arrested for trespassing." I understood the fear but there were way bigger crimes.

"Matt will figure it out. The answers might come to you," Ivy said.

An employee came out from the back. "Dr. Oscar, great. Let's try your dress on. We have your shoes, too."

I went into the dressing room and slipped on the dress. It was silky and a bit sexy for a wedding. Nothing too bad but there were a lot of sequins. The heels were high and equally dazzling.

After checking myself from every angle, I walked out for the inspection of others.

The shrieking over my appearance was all good, but it took me back to the home where I'd confronted Eli and those women shrieking in the kitchen. Bad things kept happening but that didn't mean you kept pushing all the happiness down the road for someday.

"Gorgeous," Ivy gushed.

"A little work on her makeup and hair is all she needs," the other bridesmaid said.

"Nails too, but this is a fitting. Looks good, not too tight or loose," Ivy said.

The seamstress knelt and checked the hem with the heels. Then she inspected me closely. I didn't think about my weight all the time. I was a solid size twelve or fourteen, depending on the clothing manufacturer. I had curves, big deal. But now I wondered had I gained or lost. So silly for a dress I'd wear one day and probably donate.

"We could take it in a tad here but I wouldn't. A minor fluctuation and it might feel a bit tight," the seamstress said.

"Better to leave it. She retains a bit of water and it might be uncomfortable," Ivy said.

"Lovely," I said.

"You want it tight?" Ivy asked.

"No, I think it's fine," I said.

"Okay. I'll just adjust the hem a bit for the shoes. Won't take a minute." The seamstress pinned the hem and I was able to change back into my clothes.

The gown was gorgeous but rather flashy for me.

I went out and waited politely while the other brides-maid was fitted. While we waited, Ivy flipped through the clearance rack.

"You okay now?" I asked.

She nodded. "Brody offered to postpone but I want it done. I want to be married. Done."

"There's nothing wrong with giving yourself more time to plan or just not stress. If it's not Halloween, it could be New Year's Eve," I suggested.

"I could plan myself into seven themes. I just need to do it!" Ivy yanked a dress off the rack. "This would be great on you!"

It was a pale green with a delicate pattern on the hem. "It's pretty."

"Try it on," Ivy insisted.

"Ivy," I grumbled.

"Come on. A spare dress and it's under one hundred

dollars. Good deal. Never know when you'll need it," she said.

I sighed and humored the bride. I wore my own flat shoes for it but couldn't say I hated the look.

When I stepped out, Ivy nearly burst into tears. "You have to have that. It's so you."

I didn't feel like a light sage gauzy gown was me but apparently it worked. "Why not?"

The seamstress beamed. "I'll just check the hem. Want to wear it with heels?"

"No, flats are good," I said.

Everyone in the room gave me the stink eye.

"I want a dress where I can wear flats or sandals. It'll triple the chances of me wearing it," I said.

Ivy held up her hands like she was the Roman Emperor about to issue a decree.

"Paul is tall enough for her to wear heels but not that much taller than her. I see where she's coming from. We must consider our escorts," Ivy said.

The women all accepted this as a good reason for it. I just liked flats better but I wasn't about to argue. Paul wasn't like most guys who were upset about being upstaged or if their girlfriend was too tall. I was lucky.

"See, I love that smile." Ivy hugged me.

I hadn't realized I was smiling. "I was thinking how lucky I am to have Paul."

"Aww," the other women gushed.

"You keep us in mind for your wedding, my dear." The seamstress pinned the hem on my extra gown. "Just a bit to take in at the shoulders. This material has more give."

I nodded. "Thanks." At least some little good things were

happening, and Ivy seemed far more centered and reasonable.

Did her letting go of the warehouse idea have anything to do with it? Maybe it had been just wedding nerves and once the big decisions were made she was able to manage her stress level better?

"Don't forget, bachelorette party tomorrow night!" Ivy clapped. "You can't wear that, though. It's too proper. But we can get really drunk and party because the wedding is still a week away."

The bridesmaid whooped. I had booked a limo so I could have a drink or two but I wasn't wild enough for this party. Drunk or not…

"Can't wait!" I gave my best fake smile, relieved that I wasn't in charge of this one. The other bridesmaids partied harder than I did so it was their show. The engagement party had been wild enough.

Chapter Nine

I'D SPRUNG for the limo and planned my outfit. That was all I was allowed to do for the bachelorette party. I wasn't the party girl and I was good with that.

"What's on the agenda for today?" I asked Frankie as he came downstairs for coffee.

He shrugged. "Houses. I might take you up on that loan."

"Not a loan," I said.

"Whatever. If I find the right place, I think I could enjoy this," he said.

"More than marketing?" I teased.

He shrugged. "College. You know how the parents were. Construction never would've passed muster."

"True. Do what you like. The demons and ghosts will follow you, like it or not." I finished my bagel and debated more coffee.

"Any news on the people from the warehouse?" Frankie asked.

I shook my head. "Matt went in early. I want to help but

I don't know what to do. I didn't get a feel for any of the victims or how to track them."

"You just do…stuff. So, do it," Frankie said.

"I don't have anything. No names or pictures. I need something to go on." I shrugged. "I'm not omnipotent."

"Fine. Ask Matt. Someone must've given a name for those people. Ask the blind lady," Frankie suggested.

"Maybe." I frowned.

"What?" he asked.

"I'll try Matt first. See if he got names or anything. I don't want her to influence me in any direction," I said.

Frankie's phone binged. "Good luck. See you later, I have to go meet Darla."

"You guys are spending a lot of time together," I said.

"Yeah," Frankie answered.

"Business or pleasure?" I asked.

"Both, sort of." Frankie shrugged. "Don't be so nosy."

With Frankie gone, I had the house to myself. I could go down to the police station but if there was something to track with, Matt would've told me. Tracking down family took longer with the homeless and I couldn't make it worse.

Gunner walked into the back door.

"Hey," he said.

"Hi, stranger."

"Sorry. What's up?" he asked.

"I need you to go with me to a crime scene. Keep me out of trouble." I headed upstairs for my purse and a jacket.

Half an hour later, we were at the warehouse. The crime scene tape was down and we just walked right in.

"What are we looking for?" Gunner asked.

"I just need to get a read on things. Be where they were." I sat on the floor and closed my eyes.

The dead people couldn't help. The reorientation to Heaven took time and they were too mentally scattered. I focused on the living who were taken by force and tried to tap into one.

"Both were younger and on some drug. Whatever they were given las night was different. Spiked to be worse. Knocked them out for longer," I said.

Gunner had his cell phone out and recording the info I was giving. "Got it."

"One was female, the other male. Both younger. Avoiding their families." I felt blocked but couldn't blame the witch doctor this time. Unless he'd done something to the people or the place they were now. At least it wasn't me.

"Can you sense them now?"

"Not the male. The female is groggy. Like she's still drugged." I rubbed my neck.

"Is she in danger?"

"Yes. She's cold on a metal table. People are poking and prodding her. She's terrified." I channeled but refused to feel what she was feeling or I'd lose my control.

"Sounds like an alien abduction," Gunner commented.

"It's on earth, sorry." I smirked.

"Where?" he asked.

"She doesn't know." I took a deep breath. "She's having trouble breathing. There are others around there. Someone brought another woman back from a scary room."

"Scary room?" Gunner prompted.

"That's what she thought of it as. She's afraid they'll take her in there," I explained.

"Can you get anything from the woman she's looking at? What happened to her?" Gunner asked.

I braced myself for the worst. If it was sex trafficking, it could be horrid.

As I focused on the other woman, I felt the ground under me shake. She wasn't there. She was gone.

"Are they in a van? There's not enough room," I said.

"Why do you think they're in a van?" Gunner asked.

I shook my head. "They're on the move. No wonder the police can't find them."

"Do you know where they are generally?" he asked.

"Still in Louisiana, I believe," I said.

The connection failed as the girl passed out.

"Anything else?"

"It's gone. She's unconscious. We should go share this with Matt but it's not much," I said.

"If they settle in one place, you'll get more. Don't rush or force it," Gunner said.

"You sound like me advising Frankie," I teased.

Gunner smiled. "Let's go see Matt."

"Lunch with your boyfriend? Want me to have something else to do?" I asked.

He shrugged. "Your call but you should nap this afternoon. Ivy's party is going to wear you out."

"Good point. Food and a preemptive nap," I declared.

THE SILVER LIMO DROPPED US AT A CLUB WITH MALE dancers. I felt like I was the chaperone but they'd already drained the limo of champagne and I'd only had a couple glasses.

We had a table reserved and Ivy wore a bride's tiara.

"You look nice!" Ivy shouted as we waited for the show to begin and the waiter to come around.

"Thanks!" I replied.

I'd gone with black leggings and a shimmery silver tunic over it. I was still the tamest dressed—others were in fabulous gowns and heels. I'd made sure to put on enough jewelry so I didn't feel underdressed.

"Now why hasn't Paul proposed yet?" Ivy asked.

I rolled my eyes. "Tonight is all about you," I said.

"I know but I want info. Is something wrong? I know he's not used to your powers and that's a big adjustment." Ivy leaned in.

She was a bit drunk but totally serious.

I sighed. "I'm not in a rush. He seems to be inching to it."

"He has a ring," Ivy announced.

I stared at my friend and felt her out. She wasn't lying.

"You've seen this ring?" I asked.

"Brody has. He told me not to tell you but you don't react well to true surprises. I figured you probably had a feeling anyway. Heads up," she grinned.

"Do you know when?" I asked.

She shook her head. "No, no idea. He's choosing his moment and your life is always roller coaster crazy."

"True." I sat back.

Ivy leaned in closer. "I shouldn't have told you."

I shook my head. "It's fine. I felt like we were getting closer."

"What are you going to say?" Ivy asked.

"He should get the answer before you do. He also has to ask first," I said.

"Tease," Ivy said.

I smiled. "Enjoy your night."

The lights dimmed.

"Here we go!" Mary Lou shouted with a stack of ones in her hand.

I shook my head as the show started. I had plenty to ponder while the hot men danced. Wedding traditions were weird.

I didn't need an engagement party and definitely didn't need to do this. A small wedding was enough. Too much flash and it felt like trying too hard—but that was me. This was all about Ivy!

Chapter Ten

ABOUT NOON the next day I had a cat pouncing at my toes. I'd fallen asleep in my clothes whenever we made it home. My head hurt, not from a hangover but the loud music and lighting shows that went along with the performances.

I sat up slowly and my throat felt like sandpaper. I reached for my water bottle and the cat hopped on my stomach.

"Bathroom it is." I flipped the cat off of me and rubbed her belly a little to escape.

It took a little longer than normal but I made it downstairs looking like myself.

"Fun night?" Greg teased.

"Loud. I'm too old to party like that," I admitted.

He chuckled. "Mary Lou is hungover."

"She needed to party." I downed a cup of coffee and poured another. "I need to find those people. Did you talk to Eli?"

Greg shook his head. "The guy is dodging me."

"A priest? Dodging you? Is this guy on priest probation? What sort of person did you bring around?" I asked.

"I worked outside of the rules myself," Greg said.

I popped a bagel in the toaster. "You've never scared me with a possession. I rely on you."

"Eli is young. When I was younger, things weren't as easy. I'm trying to set an example but he seems to lack any patience or quiet."

"Not good for fighting evil. He wants to run into it like a war." I grabbed butter from the fridge as the bagel popped up. "Have you checked on the women from that support group?"

Greg nodded. "I did and I put someone else in charge of the group. It's good for this group to check in with each other and keep tabs to see if anyone is having issues."

"I can see that." I focused on my bagel and coffee and felt better. "I need to find the people who were taken."

"You have a few days until the wedding. Get your dress. Don't act like Matt and the police can't do their job. I'm hearing it's probably sex trafficking," Greg said.

"Doesn't mean I can't help find them. Tracking is one thing I do well. Not a new gift."

"We don't know the whole picture."

"And the homeless aren't the biggest priority. Not a lot of family clamoring for answers. I can't even get a personal item to connect to." I finished my bagel and coffee.

"The space didn't help?" Greg asked.

"So many people. I tried. But maybe there's another way?" I nodded and left the kitchen after putting away the butter and leaving my dishes in the sink for the houseboy.

Straight out the front door, I walked to Mary Lou's mansion and rang the bell.

A young woman, one of Mary Lou's charges, answered the door.

"Hi. Mary Lou is still in bed," she said.

"Hi, that's okay. I need to see Yvette," I said.

"Right, you live across the street. She's in the sunroom." The girl let me in.

"Thanks." I headed back and found Yvette sitting in the sun. "Morning."

"This is the best shelter ever," the blind old woman said her creaky voice.

"It's more of a halfway house for young women. I'm sure we can find a better place for you to call home. More people your own age," I suggested.

She arched an eyebrow. "You came over here to talk about that now? What happened to those people in the warehouse?"

"I don't know. I can't get a read on them. I was hoping you've got some clues. Or maybe just touching you while you focus on them might help me pinpoint them. They don't seem to have family," I said.

"Which is why no one really cares." She folded her arms and her mouth turned down.

"That's not true. People care. Matt cares. I care. But no one has last names or photos. It's so much harder with so little to go on."

"That man Malek is in on it." She frowned.

I nodded. "I believe you. Maybe he's getting a cut of the people they take. I don't know anything for sure yet, but are you willing to let me try?"

"I can't see. I don't know what they looked like. I barely know the guy they took," she admitted.

I sat next to her on the wicker sofa. "I get it. I just want to try. If we find one of them, odds are they aren't the only people taken. There could be large groups of innocent people being held against their will. It's not in our control but I can try to help."

She sighed. "The cops seem to listen to you, at least."

"They do. Would you prefer we do this at the police station? Send them right away?" I asked.

"They'd think you're crazy," she said.

"Already do. Come on, I'll drive," I teased.

"Smart." She pulled out a cane and started for the front door.

In an interview room at the station, I sat with Yvette and asked some basic questions. Matt sat across from us as a witness. I felt dumb but that was nothing new.

"We locked down the warehouse again. People were getting in," Matt said.

"Sorry but I had to try. Any family come forward?" I asked.

"Nothing for those missing. The dead had some people claim their bodies but without pics or full names, it's hell trying to identify people. Also, some aren't convinced they didn't just move on to stay elsewhere," Matt replied.

Yvette snapped her cane on the floor. "Please, I know two of them well enough at least. They didn't go off elsewhere. They had people who came to see them around the warehouse. They wouldn't just go."

"We have patrols increased around there and they are reaching out to homeless in the area just in case," Matt assured us.

I smiled. "Thanks. I know you need this room for other

things so let's try this." I settled my mind and took Yvette's hand.

"Think about the people who went missing," I said.

She muttered. "Okay."

I saw their faces but got no names. The male felt cold. That sensation of slicing pain seared through my abdomen and I wanted to double over in from the agony, but in another instant it was gone, replaced by...nothingness.

I switched to focus on the female and she was warmer, not dead, I hoped. She was scared.

"De? Anything?" Matt asked.

"The male, I believe he's dead. The female is alive but I can't find her. She doesn't know where she is. I'm trying to locate her but it's protected," I said.

Matt made a note on his pad. "Protected like guards?"

"No, black magic," Yvette said. "That witch doctor put a spell on the warehouse so I'm sure he's protecting his investment. Things got repaired but those back windows— people could always get in them. Curse or oversight?"

"We can't prove it or use black magic as a crime to charge anyone," Matt said.

The system sucked but I wasn't powerful enough to change that.

I tried breaking through whatever the hex was but nothing changed.

I let go of her arm and sat back. "Sorry. I can't pinpoint a location."

"You tried." Yvette sounded disappointed.

"I'll try again. Something else." I wasn't giving up. "I'll take you home."

"Let us know," Matt said.

"Thanks."

We walked into the hallway as Malek turned the corner from station entrance.

"What are you doing here?" I asked.

Eli walked up behind Malek.

"Dr. Oscar, your friend here said the warehouse might benefit from some ritual cleansing. Anything I can do to help stop bad behavior, kidnappings, or death I'll do," Malek said.

I glared at Eli. "No."

"Healing has to start somewhere," Eli said.

"I think you're working with him and his methods," I said.

Malek shook his head. "We'd like a police presence while the priest does his work, just in case anyone might be injured."

"Liability?" I taunted.

"You haven't saved anyone since you trespassed on my property. I have improved the locks and installed cameras. Be glad I don't have you arrested for criminal trespass." Malek folded his arms.

"I did nothing criminal," I replied.

"Evil man. It's all an act," Yvette said.

Malek ignored her and stared me down. "People will suffer because of you. Keeping people out means they're on the streets in more danger. I hope you're happy."

I tried to slip by Malek to talk to Eli. "You need to talk to Greg and get your act together. This isn't good."

"You know what's good?" Malek grabbed my arm.

Matt pulled Malek aside. "That's assault."

In that split second of contact, numbers streamed through my head. I grabbed my phone and typed them in.

Grinning, I put them in my map app. "I know where they are."

"What?" Yvette gasped.

"I know because Malek knows. I got it when he touched me." I showed the map to Matt.

"Lock him up. Let's get a SWAT team and ambulances to those coordinates. We're rolling out." Matt led the way.

"Keep Yvette here and safe," I told a uniformed officer.

"I want to see them!" Yvette demanded.

"This place is dangerous. You'll see when we bring them back," I called.

"She's lying! She tricked me!" Malek shouted as an officer handcuffed him.

"Deanna," Eli called out as he followed me.

I turned on Eli. "I told you, you can't serve two masters. Respecting people is one thing but your faith can't be two-faced. You think a witch doctor wants your kind of blessing? He was using you."

I followed Matt, who tossed me a bulletproof vest. Nothing like being right in there.

"My God is stronger. I wanted to show him the way," Eli insisted.

"That's great. But your mind is weak. Vulnerable. Did you forget about the demon I pulled off of you? That takes time to recover from. I'm not saying you can't but jumping into a demon-filled project? Not a great move." I shook my head.

"I had to help!" Eli stammered, nearly in tears with frustration.

I sighed. "I have to go. You need to call Greg. You're being tricked and falling for it. If you aren't strong, you can't help anyone else. You're only exposing yourself and other good people to bad people or feeding the bad people your faith and energy."

"I can help," he insisted.

"You're not God." I turned and walked to Matt's car.

"When did you become one of those nuns from Catholic school?" Matt joked.

"Please, save me from that. I just see people with a little power and it goes right to their heads. Politicians are bad enough but a parish priest? He's freaking me out," I said.

"If he keeps stalking and harassing you, we can get a restraining order. Forget him for now. We've got people to save literally, not just their souls." Matt smiled.

I nodded. "Finally. If we're in time."

Chapter Eleven

WE DROVE north past plenty of small towns, trailer parks, and out where places were remote. I felt that we were getting closer. The woman was in danger.

"That's it." I checked my phone. "We're right on top of it."

"Problem," Matt said.

As we pulled up, a line of big dogs started barking and pulling at their chains. Behind the line of chains was a chain link fenced yard that held another sea of dogs.

"It's like one of those animal abuse commercials with the sad songs I can't watch," I said.

"I don't think they're for show. Early alarm, starved, and aggressive. I'll call animal control. They can place them with rescues," Matt said. He got on his radio. "Rear entry clear?"

"Negative. The back opens to a huge pen of hogs. Approaching makes them charge. We'll need time to clear it. We can use shields and barrel through but many of them seem wild," replied someone on the SWAT team.

"No, that's not safe," Matt said.

"It took us forty minutes to get here. It'll take animal control as long," I argued.

Matt nodded. "At least even if I put it in urgent, it'll take time. We can put them down."

"You'll run out of bullets for the human criminals and that's just awful." Human or animal lives were precious. "I don't like that but we can't wait. Let me try something."

My phone binged and I checked my message.

"Damn, I'm supposed to meet Paul. Can you text him what's going on? Thanks." I tossed Matt my phone and stepped out of the car.

I felt the pain and fear hit me in a wave. There were a lot of people inside the house. The dogs had probably alerted them. Time was critical but if we couldn't get in the back, the bad guys couldn't get out either.

Neither could the victims.

I closed my eyes and pulled the angels in from home.

"Nice puppies," I said softly.

I walked forward confidently and the ones on chains couldn't reach me. Unlatching the gate, I exhaled all the fear. The barking was almost as loud as the club last night.

I heard a gunshot.

"De, get back here! They're shooting," Matt shouted.

Faith. If I was going to prove the witch doc and Eli wrong, I had to walk the walk.

"I'm fine," I called back. "Come on."

I left the gate open behind me but none of the dogs tried to leave the enclosure. Walking slowly, I was sniffed and licked but despite fervent barking, no one bit me. A few growled but all I had to do was look at them and it seemed to smooth it all over. "We'll get you food and water soon. I swear. Good doggies."

As I hit the porch a SWAT team, led by Matt, swarmed around me and kicked in the door.

"Stay with the dogs," Matt ordered.

I smelled death and chemicals from inside. Once the teams were inside, I peeked in the front room. It wasn't decorated like a house but more like "Dexter" or some medical show.

It wasn't human trafficking, it was organ harvesting.

"Oh God," I said.

The dogs and hogs weren't just protection. They were eating the evidence. Consuming the remains of the people once they were harvested for all possible organs.

"Wow." I stepped inside and saw the surgical instruments.

"Got 'em," one cop called.

"Alive?" Matt asked.

"Dead. They shot themselves. They weren't shooting at me," I supplied.

In a small bedroom there was a table lined with coolers.

Someone ran in from outside. "We found a small plane in the woods and a refrigerated truck. Got that locked down."

"How many people?" I asked.

"One dead. Three drugged. One is open on the table. Get the paramedics in here. We need a medivac helicopter," Matt ordered.

I went out and got my phone from the car. I texted Ivy that I'd be late for the rehearsal dinner. Sitting to one side on the porch so I wasn't in the way, I had dogs sniffing me.

"This is weird," I said.

I felt the energy between me and the animals. Normally I had someone with me. Matt was the only one here. No Ivy, no Greg, or anyone. Maybe I'd be okay without my team? They could move out. I wish my brother was here but that was for education.

My phone rang. It was Paul.

"Hi, sorry. Can you grab my dress from the shop?" I asked.

"Sure. Matt texted. You okay?" he asked.

"Yeah, I charmed a bunch of dogs that are currently sitting here staring at me. It wasn't sex trafficking," I said.

"Okay. What was it? Are they all dead?" he asked.

I smiled. "No, one is gone but some are drugged. Its organ harvesting. I can't believe they're doing so much in the middle of nowhere," I said.

"Organs are a big business. Wait lists are awful for people who need transplants," he replied.

I sighed. "And who misses some homeless people? They go missing and no one knows for sure because they could've just moved on to squat somewhere else. No family. We need to find a good place for Yvette. She's disabled and a senior."

"I've been looking into that. Don't stress. You've done enough," he said.

"Thanks. I'll see you when I get back. Bye," I said.

"Bye." He ended the call.

I saw one police officer standing guard but her phone was out, and she was recording.

I had a bad feeling.

I walked over to her. "What are you doing?"

"Documenting the entry. It's policy. We didn't fire. We didn't hurt any of the dogs. You worked a miracle with them. The Cajun dog whisperer." She smiled.

"But it's official police business?" I asked.

She nodded. "We have to be able to prove we didn't

abuse anyone. Sign of the times. You might not like being on the video but we can't help it."

"Got it." I didn't like it but I'd worked with more good cops than bad ones. If that kept the bad ones in line and protected the innocent, so much the better. "Can you send me the video once it's all over?"

"I can put in a request for a copy," she confirmed.

"Thanks." I went back to the porch and my canine minions.

My brother would want to see me playing St. Francis. "No one better ask me to multiply wine at the wedding," I muttered to myself.

I MISSED THE ACTUAL REHEARSAL BUT MADE IT TO THE DINNER at the funky Cajun place Ivy and Brody picked.

"Sorry." I hugged Ivy.

"No problem. Paul ordered for you," Ivy said.

"Thanks. Really sorry. I had to keep these dogs calm. A lot of people had to be medically moved." I felt like I'd been a bad friend.

Ivy took my hand. "I'm sorry. I've been a terrible friend and terrible bride. You were right about the warehouse. I shouldn't have pushed."

"You saved those people by bringing me there. Matt had no leads. I just wish we had a good place to take all those homeless people," I said.

Ivy nodded. "You'll figure it out. I have a lot to figure out."

"What?" I asked.

She shook her head. "Greg dragged me to church. I found a good one."

"Okay. But you've got your guy. You're great at running the clubs. Life never stops changing but you know what you're good at and you're loved. Lots of friends. Don't start second guessing things because one thing might feel different," I advised.

"Marriage. It's so huge," she said.

I nodded. "And hasn't been legal for that long. I can see where you thought you might never get here legally."

"It's not about it being gay. Just marriage," Ivy said.

"That, too." I glanced over at Paul. "Even when you think it's the right one. How do you know?"

"What am I doing?" She ignored her salad.

"Cold feet. This is why you wanted the rehearsal a couple days before the ceremony. The practice brings up nerves. You've never doubted. This is just natural. And you don't even get stage fright. Imagine people not used to all eyes on them." I shrugged.

Ivy nodded. "You're right. Go kiss your boyfriend. Marriage is wonderful."

Brody was working the room with ease, but Ivy didn't budge. This hall…well, the extended full banquet room, not the small quarter we had for this dinner, would've worked just fine for the wedding reception, if you asked me. Lovely silver and black decorations, just a touch here and there. Big round tables and good food. A limited open bar since the groom's side paid for the rehearsal dinner—ah, tradition. But people were having a good time and that's what mattered. It wasn't about showing off. One place was just as good as another.

"Okay. I'm starving." I found my seat and grabbed a roll.

"Chicken?" Paul asked.

"Good call. The dogs are all safe at a no kill sanctuary, but dry dog food doesn't compare to human remains. I hope they eat," I said.

A drag queen scrunched her face at me.

"Sorry," I said softly. I had to remember where I was. Normal people were around, not just my motley crew.

"Good thing we got salads instead of the lobster bisque," Paul teased.

"Sorry. No more organ talk." I kissed him and got some food into my system.

People in the wedding and out of town guests talked and laughed. It was a good feeling. I checked on Ivy again and she still sat there as though frozen all the way through. Were the cold feet were spreading?

"Maybe she spends so much time making things fabulous for others, she's not sure how to fully enjoy it herself? But I've seen her perform and she loves attention." It made no sense.

Paul patted my shoulder. "It'll either resolve itself with the wedding or get worse and you can step in. You're honestly too close to be objective."

"I saw when things were hanging onto you, remember?" I asked.

He smiled. "I was still newish. At least new to your inner circle. You saw me with a more critical eye. You love Ivy like a sister. You've counted on her for years. It's easy to write things off as wedding jitters or a bad day."

I looked him in the eyes. "You're saying I'm missing something?"

"No, I'm saying you could. You're too close. Greg is, too. Let's get through the wedding and see if she evens out. Marriage is a big life change. A wedding is one day but maybe she was focused just on the event and the idea of forever and married life is sinking in. That might freak her out," he suggested.

I nodded. "She does love bling and a party. Domestic life might not be her norm but I'm sure they must've talked about it."

"We haven't, really. But you can afford help, so the household stuff isn't an issue. Money fixes a lot of things, but not schedules and priorities." Paul held my hand.

He was a brilliant shrink, no doubt. "Subtle change of conversation. Wonderful. I wish I could have a schedule and control my work. You are a priority but as the casino trip proved, I can't really plan a vacation and enjoy it like normal people."

"I can handle your life as long as I know I'm part of it. Sometimes I think it's easier for you if I'm not there," he said.

I shook my head. "No, never. You work so hard between your practice and the rehabs, I don't want to drag you into something more. I want you to enjoy your life, too. I think we do need to hire someone to manage the rehabs. Our vision but take you out of the day-to-day operations."

Paul nodded. "I can cut back on my patients, too. Refer some to others."

"Only if it's safe for them," I said.

"Of course." He smiled. "But that means I'm underfoot a lot."

"I need that. You're calming. Normally, that was Ivy," I admitted.

Greg came over. "You okay?"

"Sure. You get a hold of Eli? He's playing with all the wrong people," I warned.

"Malek got arrested under suspicion of being an accomplice to the organ ring. They've actually detained Eli for questioning," Greg said.

"Good. He won't be wreaking havoc on New Orleans tonight." I grabbed another roll. "What's with Ivy and the church?"

Paul frowned but Greg nodded.

"Her parents were not the most supportive. They aren't coming. She felt rejected all over again and it hurts her. That let her be influenced by others. Probably Eli. My fault," Greg said.

"No one's fault but I don't like Eli hanging around. Frankie is new enough and two newbies is trouble." I shook my head

I caught my brother's eye and waved.

"He brought Darla," Paul commented.

I smiled. "Maybe he's got a girlfriend and a new business?" I pondered.

"He has to make it his own," Greg said.

I nodded. "I'm glad."

Mary Lou walked over. "Hey, I just reminded the couple to get their marriage license. There is a waiting period so they must get it in advance."

"How nice of you," I said.

"It got a little quiet but I said cold feet is totally normal." Mary Lou beamed. "Everything is perfect."

"You did a great job planning," I said.

"Thanks. It's so nice to have a happy event to plan. I'll do checks tomorrow. Got your dress?" she asked.

I looked at Paul.

"Picked it up today," he said.

"Thanks." I leaned my head on his shoulder.

"Okay, looks like the food is coming. Do you want to say anything tonight?" she asked.

"Speeches at the rehearsal dinner? I don't think I have anything to say," I replied.

Mary Lou nodded and winked. "This is a very freeform event. Every couple does the rehearsal dinner a little bit differently. No worries. Oh, I invited Yvette to stay with us permanently and help mentor the girls."

"That's great. I was hitting a lot of roadblocks," Paul said.

"You're a saint, Mary Lou," I said.

"I need the help and she's got a lot of stories that the girls relate to better than me. Back to work." Mary Lou waved.

She and Greg went back to their spots.

"I'm not the maid of honor," I said.

"Maybe you'll catch the bouquet," Paul teased.

"If you propose any time around Ivy's wedding, I will slap you. No stealing her thunder or big day or anything. No." I wagged a finger at him.

He grinned. "I would never upstage a drag queen. No matter how much fun it'd be to see your face."

Part of me worried that he'd pre-cleared something with Ivy to shock and surprise me. I couldn't be mad then. No, he wouldn't do that. I had to believe that.

"I'm not big on public moments," I said.

Gunner laughed from across the table. "Tell that to the internet."

Chapter Twelve

"INTERNET?" Paul pulled out his phone.

"What?" I asked.

Gunner showed the video of me approaching the dogs. There was voiceover.

"This is uncut, unedited, leaked footage from a police event today. You see her control a pack of dogs she's never met before. This psychic arrived with the police and the animals prevented the entry to rescue critically hurt people."

"That cop," I asked.

"Doesn't say who loaded it," Gunner said.

"Tell Matt do something. Get an order to take it down. It's gotta be police footage," I said.

Paul watched it. "You did do what they're saying. It's the truth. You could've been mauled to death."

I shook my head. "No, I've done things with animals before. Keeping the peace. It's fine. It's only a big deal because she's sharing the video."

Our food came and I focused on eating. I'd used up a lot of energy.

"I'll talk to Matt but someone else could've recorded you, too. Maybe someone did it on their personal phone? Cops can't do much about that stuff. Could be a security camera," Gunner said.

"Who else would record it but a cop? I didn't see anyone else. There were no neighbor's way out there. Someone should get in trouble," I said.

"For a video? That's the truth. De," Paul said.

"I heard it. I just hate these publicity blips. They've happened before. I get noticed for a bit and it all goes back to normal. Just annoying." I pouted.

Paul kissed my temple. "You saved people. You did your job. Don't worry about the rest. The great thing about New Orleans is that the people aren't easily shocked. Miracle or magic, they don't care."

I nodded. "I might need doughnuts for breakfast. Good thing we didn't take my dress in the bit the seamstress wanted to."

"You burned it off with your powers, I'm sure." Paul rubbed the back of my neck.

The soothing touch was exactly what I needed. No doubt there would be music and dancing at this rehearsal dinner. I'd be headed to bed once the formal responsibilities were done.

"Does that video have a lot of views?" I asked.

"No, forget about it," Paul said.

I rolled my eyes. "You're a bad liar."

"Want me to propose?" he taunted.

I shot him a look. "I want us to eat and I need to crash hard."

"You're the boss," he teased.

By the next morning, the video had gone officially viral.

The doorbell rang as I poured my first cup of coffee. I puttered to the door and looked before I opened it.

Paul had doughnuts. I smiled. "Thanks."

"I got some of your faves and some of mine." He kissed me as he walked in.

We settled in the kitchen and gorged on sugar and coffee.

"Better?" he asked.

I shrugged. "That video is everywhere. It's weird."

"And you didn't even tell me," Frankie said as he entered.

I rolled my eyes. "Who cares? Lots of people can control animals."

"But you can't. You don't like dogs that much. You've never trained them or worked with them." Frankie got coffee and inspected the doughnuts. "Thanks, but I'll have some yogurt."

"Make me feel unhealthy," I scolded.

He shot me a look. "I'm narrowing it down. I'll probably put an offer in on a house soon. You still want to loan me the money?"

I nodded. "I do. I want an inspection first."

"Does that include you walking through and doing a demon scan?" Frankie teased.

"No, that's your department. The haunted level and the renovation. I just want to be sure it's not full of black mold or radiation or something weird," I replied.

"Deal." He reached out a hand.

"Deal." I shook it. "So, are you and Darla a thing?"

He scoffed but didn't look me in the eye. I didn't buy it but didn't push.

"She is an heiress in her own right. That's a fancy plantation. Not cheap to maintain, but if they ever sold it…" Paul said.

Frankie blushed and walked away. "Please, she doesn't even live there. Call if you need anything but I think you earned the day off."

"Thanks, happy house hunting," I called to Frankie but grinned at Paul.

"I have the feeling we're going to research Darla a bit more," Paul said.

"Maybe. Not today. The wedding is coming too fast. I need a day off. Tomorrow is nails and stuff." I sighed.

"That's grueling," he teased.

"Got your suit ready?" I asked. Men had it so easy.

He nodded. "Always. What do you want to do on your day off?"

I realized that it was Sunday. He was off of work and I didn't need to go chasing down kidnapped people today.

"Whatever you want. As long as we're together. No work," I said.

"You got it." He refilled our coffee.

Matt arrived home to find Paul and I doing something we never did. Nothing. Well, sitting on the couch watching TV with nothing else distracting us.

"Cozy," Matt teased.

"How'd it go?" I asked.

"Malek is standing his ground and refusing to confess

but they're combing his financial records for proof that he got kickbacks from the organ theft," Matt said.

"And the video?" I went to my main concern.

Matt sat down in a chair off to the side near the fireplace. "You've handled animals before. It's not new."

"That's not the point," I replied.

"Any media attention always spikes and dies down. People are so distracted today that unless you're out there posting like a Kardashian, no one will remember you in a week," he said.

"Good. But she can take the video down," I held my ground.

"It's not the official police video. It's security camera footage. Clearly that shack is a place they've used to harvest organs before and whoever is in charge of this ring likes to keep an eye on things. They realized at the last minute we were coming but our force was so big people chose arrest over death by police or being chased down." Matt paused to rub a hand across his forehead. "As for the video, it only looked like that officer posted the footage. Someone hacked her social media account," Matt explained.

"Why?" I asked.

Matt shrugged. "To set her up, I'm assuming. She wanted to ask you a question. A favor. She was talking about you working miracles and I think a colleague didn't care for her admiration of you and wanted to teach her a lesson. Anyway, we're dealing with that with an internal investigation. Whoever has the security footage, there's no way to prove it's illegally obtained. It's their property. It's already trending down."

"What about this woman who wanted a favor?" Paul asked.

"She's had a few miscarriages. She wants you to help." Matt looked incredibly uncomfortable.

I frowned. "I'm really not equipped for that. Not that kind of doctor."

Matt laughed. "I think she means work your miracles."

"No," I said.

Matt sighed. "Be a conduit for the healing. Whatever. You could try."

I rolled my eyes. "Maybe. Let it die down right now. I don't want to feel like I'm backed into a corner."

"You won't help?" Paul asked.

"I can try but right now I'm feeling used and tapped. I need to get stronger and more centered," I said.

Matt nodded. "I'll give her your number. You two can hash it out."

"After the wedding. Don't promise her contact any sooner. I need to finish what I've started, and it has to be private. I'm not looking for public recognition." I shrugged. It wasn't in my hands. None of it. I'd done nothing to get the visions or any other gifts. I could put every effort in healing her or helping her, but it was really up to her faith and the big man upstairs.

Chapter Thirteen

WEDDINGS WERE happy events but I was fighting the feeling that Eli or the witch doctor was going to crash or make a mess of things. Malek wasn't poor and bail had to have been set by now.

I dressed for the day and went down.

Mary Lou gasped. "You look amazing."

I laughed. "Thanks. What needs to be done?"

"Not a thing. The decorations are done. The tables and canopy are out. The ceremony area is ready to go. Four hours to go." Mary Lou nodded.

"Brody is good at your place?" I asked.

"Yes, Greg and the other groomsmen are getting him ready. I'm letting Ivy sleep a bit because she was nervous last night but I should go and wake her. The other bridesmaids are due here any minute," Mary Lou said.

"Okay, I'll answer the door or whatever." I shrugged.

"Matt is across the street. Gunner is out back keeping an eye on the setup. Okay. Perfect. You've got the door covered. See you in a bit." Mary Lou went upstairs.

I went to the kitchen for some coffee and passed Frankie sitting outside the door that led to the storage area under the stairs.

"What's going on?" I asked.

"I can feel the haunted objects. The curses," he said.

I smiled. "Your powers are growing. But we have a wedding today."

"I put an offer in on a house. I might need the cash," he said.

"Sure. But today is a wedding and Halloween, so no work. I might need your help keeping an eye out for Eli or Malek. I don't want them crashing or causing trouble." I tapped him on the shoulder.

"Sure. Right. On it." He stood up with a smile.

"Darla coming as your plus one?" I asked.

Frankie grinned bigger. "Yeah. I should change into my suit. You look awesome. I'll be down in a few."

I filled a travel mug with coffee to minimize any spilling. Of course, the doorbell rang just then. I made my way to the door, still in bare feet because I wasn't wearing those heels until I had to.

It wasn't the bridesmaids.

Paul looked extra handsome in a black suit that bordered on a modern tux but not quite.

"You look nice," I teased.

"Just nice? I overpaid." He kissed me.

"Easy, this is wedding makeup." I had done multiple layers of foundation and concealer. Digital photos didn't hide much.

"Oh please." He followed me back to the kitchen and poured his own coffee. "Seems quiet. I'm early."

"Yeah, the last-minute crazy will hit in a couple hours, I'm sure." I pondered breakfast.

Mary Lou's heels clicked down the stairs.

"How's Ivy? Bridezilla?" I teased.

When she turned the corner into the kitchen, Mary Lou looked like she'd seen a ghost.

"What's wrong?" Paul asked.

"She's gone." Mary Lou handed me a note.

"Gone?" I hadn't felt her leave. "Cold feet?"

"I guess. She says she'll text us but she's not ready to talk." Mary Lou looked around. "We have guests and food."

"Someone has to tell Brody." I had a feeling I knew who had sabotaged things.

Our phones started chiming. The text had arrived.

Ivy: *Sorry, I can't. I know I've been up and down lately. Whatever caused it, I need to be sure I'm doing things for the right reasons. I'm really sorry but I need to be alone for a bit. Don't hate me but please don't contact me. I'll reach out when I'm ready.*

"Holy crap," Paul said.

"Greg has to know where she is," I said as I turned to go across the street.

Paul held my arm. "No. If he does, he'll handle it. You can't fix everything for everyone."

"She's my friend. How did I not see her freaking out? She was fine last night." What had I missed?

"It's not about you. She made a choice. If she's not ready, she's not." Paul shrugged.

I looked to Mary Lou. "Maybe it felt like too much. Cold feet can turn into pressure and fear for others. Real fear. It's not like Ivy ever had trouble being the center of attention."

"I swear Malek and Eli did something to her." I called Greg.

"I don't know where she is," he answered immediately. "Brody is coming over to get his stuff."

"What? He doesn't have to leave," I said.

"Talk to him. I'm trying to reach Ivy," Greg replied.

I took a deep breath. "You need to pin down Eli and Malek and make sure they didn't curse Ivy or something."

"What?" Greg asked.

"You heard me. Eli was judging a gay wedding and Malek was annoyed Ivy wanted to rent the place. Who is annoyed about someone giving them money? He didn't want his operation to be found out and we did anyway. He's pissed," I said.

"Matt and I will look into that. Cancel the wedding," he said.

"We have less than four hours. How can we cancel the wedding? The food and all of that is already in process. They'll lose their deposits. I can cover that but it's such a waste." I couldn't focus on what to worry about first.

"De, relax. It's her choice," Greg said.

I hung up and couldn't believe it.

Brody walked in. "Sorry about all this."

He looked more angry than hurt but was quiet.

"Brody, you don't have to move out. Ivy had a rough time but you'll work it out," I said. "You're good for her."

He nodded. "I don't get what happened. I need to pack a bag. We have a hotel room for tonight anyway. Too late to cancel. I can stay there and figure things out in the morning."

"You shouldn't be alone," Mary Lou said.

Brody stomped up the stairs.

"I know why the bridesmaids aren't here," Mary Lou sighed. "What do I do?"

"Give me a minute with De," Paul said.

Mary Lou's eyes twinkled.

"What? Why?" I asked as Mary Lou left.

"I wasn't going to do this today. I promise. Well, maybe after the reception. Not to steal anyone's thunder." Paul pulled a ring from his pocket.

It wasn't huge but delicate and looked antique.

"It's not even in a box. And now?" I asked.

He chuckled. "It's an old family ring. It'll have to be sized. But yes, now. If we plan a wedding, you might freak out and run. Let's just borrow theirs."

"What?" I laughed. "Today? That's crazy."

"Want me to kneel down?" he asked.

"No, I want to you use your brain. We don't have a license or someone to marry us. Greg is some online minister, not legit church anymore. He'll be worried about Ivy. I'm supposed to get married without Ivy?" I had a million reasons but I wanted to say yes.

"We can record it. Facetime your parents. It's not that crazy," he said.

I folded my arms. "License. It won't be legal."

"We can get one. It's a party. Why waste the food, the DJ, and the decorations? It's not exactly us but our lives get co-opted by others all the time. Why not co-opt this and it's done? I'm sure," he said.

He knelt down.

I was sure he was the one. "I just don't know about stealing someone's wedding."

"Is that a yes?" he pressed.

"Yes, get up. Damn, you're stubborn. We just can't." I hugged him when he stood.

"Good, that's part one. Two, we get the license." He put the ring on my finger. It was a little loose but not much.

Frankie walked in. "What's up with that text?"

"Ivy got cold feet. I think your sis and I should just get married. What do you think?" Paul asked.

"Don't ask him. What are you doing?" I smacked his arm.

Frankie noticed the ring. "Engaged. Really? Cool. Sure. We're all primed for a wedding. I'll give the bride away."

"No, no one is giving me away. I'm not a used car. What the hell are you people thinking? No license. There is a waiting period even if we got one." I wagged a finger at them.

Paul smiled. "You realize Matt is a highly-placed cop. He might know a judge or two that can waive that waiting period."

Frankie grinned. "I'll get Matt. You get your document for the license thing. We'll meet you there."

"My wedding anniversary is going to be Halloween?" I asked.

Paul put his arm around me. "Why not? It's so you. We'll never forget it."

It all happened so fast and I hadn't seen any of it coming. I opened my mouth to comment but closed it. There were no words because I wasn't hating any of it.

"Look, if you really want to we'll wait. Get your parents here in person or other friends, I get it. We can wait. But I was waiting for a sign. Waiting for the right time and it happened. Don't do it for me. Do it because it feels right," he said.

"Now that's the most persuasive thing you've ever said. I'll run upstairs and get the papers I need. We can swing by your place. Oh crap. You can move in here. Maybe Brody can sublet your place?" I suggested.

"Priorities, hon. We're on a clock for the wedding guests," he said.

I smirked. "I'm the wife, I can make you wait all day. Complain as much as you want."

"To be the wife, you need the license," he reminded me.

"Men," I muttered.

THREE HOURS LATER, I'D SWAPPED THE RED DRESS FOR THE funky light green one and white flats. Not quite bridal but close enough.

I was retouching my makeup when someone knocked on the door.

"Who is it?" Mary Lou snapped.

"Greg," came the reply.

"Come in," I said.

Greg entered. "No word from Ivy. Malek is still in town, legally he can't leave out on bail. Matt is having him watched. They're investigating every bank account and his phone records. Sounds like they're building a huge case of him profiting off of the homeless for that organ harvesting ring. It's a big break. Malek won't bother us."

"He already has. He messed with Ivy," I said.

"You don't know that for sure," Mary Lou said.

"Someone did," I countered.

Greg nodded. "That's the thing. Eli is missing. Gone. None of the monks or anyone in his assigned parish can find him. I got a text from him just now."

"Oh no," I said.

"He's with Ivy. I don't know why or how. I don't know if

he's following her or they're together, but he told me not to worry about her. He'll take care of her," Greg said.

"That's a threat. We need to get Matt on it. Get a warrant to pull his travel records and go find them," I said.

"I'm going to let Matt know. I should've waited until after the wedding but I wanted to be honest. Maybe you can sense where she is?" he asked.

"I've been trying. She's either blocked, blocking me, or something is interfering. Like Eli or Malek," I said.

Greg nodded. "Matt is going to get to work on it. See how far he can get. But the most dangerous part is Eli really believes he's helping people."

"Get Ivy to tell us where she is. She'll listen to you," I said.

"I've tried. If I text her that you borrowed her wedding and are getting married, it might get her to talk," Greg pointed out.

I paced the room. "I should call it all off. It's wrong to get married when my friend is in danger."

"She's not. Not if she's texting me back. I think she can take care of herself. Whatever it is, she knows where we are. She can ask for help." Greg looked at me. "You're gorgeous. Get married unless you don't want to. Your life is always a mess of other people's needs. Paul was smart to jump on this. There will always be a case or a problem."

"Ivy is a friend, not a problem," I shot back.

"And you have a photographer and a guy shooting very professional video. She can see it later. She bailed on us. Stop putting yourself last," Greg said.

"Any of the monks here?" I asked.

He nodded. "Why?"

"I might want a real blessing. I mean, I know the judge

has to sign off on the waiver. And you're here but…" That sounded bad.

"I'm not officially with the church anymore," Greg said. "I'll ask them."

"Thanks." I smiled.

"Ten minutes to showtime. Greg, make sure Paul and Frankie are in place, please. Go." Mary Lou waved at him to leave.

I HAD ONE OF THE SHORTEST ENGAGEMENTS EVER BUT ONCE I was there in front of a monk, a judge, and Greg…but the vows were traditional, and our wedding bands were borrowed from Gran's old jewelry box. We'd figure that out later.

The DJ had to adjust his plan and some of the guests didn't stay because of the changeup but most stayed. A few other people showed up to a last-minute invite.

"Okay?" Paul asked during our first dance.

I smiled. "I'm good. Oddly calm."

"You didn't run off," he teased.

"I'm worried about Ivy but I don't think she's being held against her will. If she needs time—that's what she needs." I felt bad for Brody. He hadn't attended the wedding. He'd left and not replied to texts.

"Where should we honeymoon?" he asked.

I rolled my eyes. "You planned time off?"

Paul frowned. "No, so we need to plan something."

"I don't get to plan. I'll try my best," I said.

Paul kissed me. The cheers made my face burn red.

"I know what I got myself into," he said.

My life never went as planned but this was a nice surprise.

"I'm not changing my name," I tossed out there.

My hubby just smiled. "I know. Tish might need a cat bed since I'm evicting her."

"Good luck with that." I grinned back at him.

Don't miss Book 10~~~Available Now!

A Boat, A Banshee, and a Breakdown

A Personal Note from Ivy...

Dear Beloved Reader,

I have to apologize. Even De didn't see that coming...

Brody is so mad. I'm so shocked. Pearl is hurt that he wasn't the ring bearer.

And I missed De's wedding on top of it all! What a horrible friend I am. Please don't give up on me... I promise I'll have a fabulous wedding one day. At least De had a beautiful garden wedding like she wanted.

I'll be back soon. I could never abandon our loyal readers. But I might not be the life of the party every day. That's a big job.

Kisses from Europe!
  Ivy Delacroix

PS: If you missed books, the titles are listed below!

    Book 1: A Mansion, A Drag Queen, And A New Job

    Book 2: A Club, An Imposter, And A Competition

    Book 3: A Bar, A Brother, And A Ghost Hunt

    Book 4: A Voodoo Shop, A Zombie, And A Party

    Book 5: A Cemetery, A Cannibal, and the Day of the Dead

    Book 6: A Dungeon, A Vampire, and an Infatuation

    Book 7: A Casino, A Cheater, and a Charity Ball

    Book 8: A Plantation, A Tour Guide, and a Poltergeist

    Book 9: A Warehouse, A Witch Doctor, and a Wedding

About the Author

A loyal Chicago girl who loves deep dish pizza, the Cubs, and The Lake, CC Dragon is fascinated by the metaphysical and paranormal. She loves creating characters, especially amateur sleuths who solve mysteries. A coffee and chocolate addict who loves fast cars, she's still looking for a hero who likes to cook and clean...so she can write more!

Keep in touch:
Website:
www.authorccdragon.com

Facebook:
https://www.facebook.com/ccdragonauthor

Facebook Group:
https://www.facebook.com/groups/752998138081518/

Google +:
http://tinyurl.com/ccdragong

Twitter:
https://twitter.com/authorccdragon

69174004R00086

Made in the USA
Columbia, SC
13 August 2019